Go ahead and scream.

No one can hear you. You're no longer in the safe world you know.

You've taken a terrifying step . . .

into the darkest corners of your imagination.

You've opened the door to . . .

the NIGHTMARE room

Liar Liar

R.L. STINE

AVON BOOKS
An Imprint of HarperCollinsPublishers

PARACHUTE PRESS

Welcome...

I'm R.L. Stine. Let me introduce you to Ross Arthur. He's that boy with straight, brown hair and a slightly crooked smile, talking to two girls by the swimming pool.

You might say that Ross has everything. He's popular, smart, and good looking. His father is an exec for a big movie studio. Ross lives in Beverly Hills with a swimming pool and tennis courts in his backyard.

A perfect life? Not quite.

Ross has a little problem. He constantly tells stories. Some people might call them lies. In fact, Ross has told so many lies to so many people, it's hard for him to tell what's real and what isn't.

Ross's little problem is about to take him to a frightening place—The Nightmare Room. And once he's inside, Ross is going to make a terrifying discovery—you can't talk your way out!

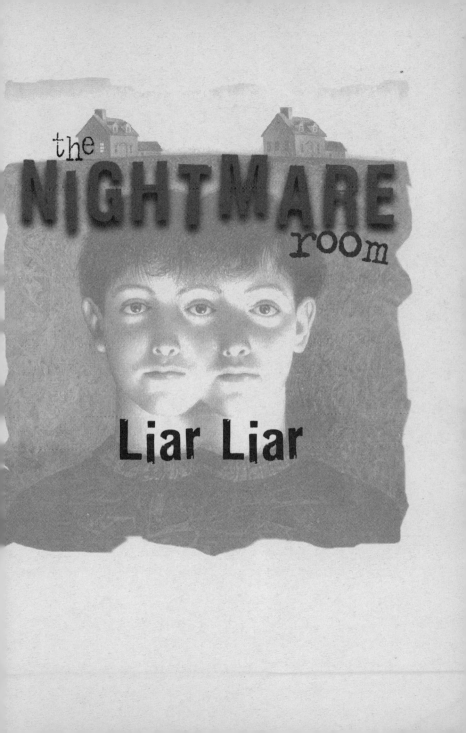

the NiGHTMARE room

Liar Liar

When I was little, a kid told me that everyone has an exact double somewhere in the world. I told the kid he was crazy.

I'm twelve now. And I just saw my exact double. Of course, I didn't believe my eyes. He didn't just look like me—he was me!

I wasn't staring into a mirror. I was staring at a boy with my face—my straight, brown hair, my blue eyes, my sort-of crooked smile. My FACE! My BODY! I was staring at ME! ME!

I know, I know. I sound a little crazed.

But you'd be crazed too if you had an exact double, and you didn't know who he was or where he came from.

I'm going to take a deep breath. That's what my dad always tells me to do. "Take a deep breath, Ross," he says.

My dad is a studio exec—one of the bosses at Mango Pictures. He spends his day arguing with movie producers, directors, and movie stars. He says he takes about a million deep breaths a day. It helps keep him calm.

So, I'm going to take a deep breath. And I'm going to start my story at the beginning. Or maybe a little before the beginning.

By the way, I lied about the blue eyes.

I don't have blue eyes. Actually, they're dark gray. Which is almost blue—right?

I guess I'll start my story at school. I go to Beverly Hills Middle School, which is only a few blocks from my house.

I know what you're thinking. I'm so lucky to have a dad in the movie business and live in a big house in Beverly Hills with a swimming pool and a tennis court, and our own screening room in the basement.

You're right. It's lucky. I'm very lucky. But I still have problems. Lots of problems.

The other morning Cindy Matson was my problem. I ran into Cindy in the hall between classes, and I could see she was really steamed. Her face was red, and she kept tugging at her black bangs, then clenching and unclenching her fists. Tense. Extremely tense.

"Ross—where were you?" she asked, blocking my way.

Cindy is taller than I am. She's at least seven or eight feet tall. And she works out. She could be a stuntwoman for *Xena: Warrior Princess*. So I try to stay on her good side.

"Uh . . . where was I?" I thought it might be safe to repeat the question.

But Cindy exploded anyway. "Remember? You were going to meet me? We were going to Urban Outfitters together yesterday afternoon?"

"Yes, I know," I said. "But you see . . . " I had to think quickly. "My tennis lesson got switched. Because my regular instructor hurt his hand. He was trying to open one of those cans of tennis balls. And his hand got stuck, and he sprained his wrist. Really. So my lesson got moved. And my racket was being restrung. So I had to go to the tennis shop on Wilshire and get a loaner."

I stopped to breathe. Was she buying that excuse? No.

"Ross, that is *so* not true," Cindy said, rolling her eyes. "Your tennis lessons are on Saturday. Can't you ever just tell the truth? You forgot about me—right? You just forgot."

"No way," I insisted. "Actually, what happened was . . . the truth. The total truth. My dog got sick, and Mom asked me to help take him to the vet. And so I—"

"When did you get a dog?" Cindy interrupted.

"Huh?" I stared at the floor, thinking hard. She was right. We don't have a dog.

Sometimes I work so hard on these stories, I mess up some of the details.

Cindy rolled her eyes for about the thousandth time. "You do remember that you're going with me to Max's pool party Friday night—don't you?"

I had completely forgotten.

"Of course," I said. "No way I'd forget that."

The bell rang. We were both late for class.

We turned and jogged off in different directions. I turned a corner—and bumped into Sharma Gregory.

Sharma is tiny and blond and speaks in a mousy whisper. She is the anti-Cindy. She's very pretty, and she's a true brainiac. Last April she won a trip to Washington, D.C., because of an essay she wrote. (But she didn't go because she was invited to a really cool Oscar party.)

"Hey, Ross—" She pointed at me. "Max's party Friday night—right?"

I grinned at her. "Yeah. For sure."

"Should I meet you there, or do you want to come over to my house first?"

Oh, wow. I'd also asked Sharma to go with me to the party!

Why did I invite her? She'd let me copy off her chemistry test. So I thought I'd give her a break.

"Uh . . . I'll meet you there," I said. I flashed her a thumbs-up and hurried into English class.

I closed the classroom door carefully behind me and tiptoed to my seat. I hoped Miss Douglas wouldn't notice I was late. Luckily, my seat is in the back row, so it's easy to sneak in and out.

"Ross, you're late," Miss Douglas called.

"Uh . . . yeah," I said, tugging my notebook from my backpack. Think fast, Ross. "I had to stay late in Mr. Harrison's class and . . . uh . . . help him return some books to the library. Mr. Harrison meant to give me a late pass, but he forgot."

Miss Douglas nodded. I think she believed me.

"If you will all take out your essays," she said, straightening the books on her desk. She's always lining up the things on her desk, making them perfectly straight.

"I'd like for some of you to share your essays with the class. Why don't we start with you, Ross?" She flashed me a toothy grin. Her gums show when she smiles.

"Uh . . . share my essay?" I had to stall for time. Had to think fast.

I started the essay last night. Well, actually, I started to think about starting the essay. But then *WWF Smackdown* came on. And by the time it was over, it was time to go to bed.

Miss Douglas's grin faded. "Do you have your essay, Ross?"

"Well, I wrote it," I told her. "But it's still in my computer. Because we had some kind of electrical backup or something at my house. And my printer blew up! Smoke was pouring out of it like a toaster. So I couldn't print what I wrote. But I'm getting a new printer after school. So I'll bring it in tomorrow."

Good one, huh?

At least, I thought it was good. But before I knew it, Miss Douglas swept down the aisle until she stood right over me.

She gazed down at me sternly through her red-rimmed glasses. "Ross," she said through gritted teeth. "Listen to me. Be careful. If you keep this up, you may fail this course."

I stared back at her. "Keep what up?" I asked.

I hurried to my locker after school. Some guys wanted to hang out, but I couldn't. I knew my dad was waiting outside to drive me to my acting class.

Dad isn't thrilled about my acting lessons. But Jerry Nadler, my teacher, is an old friend of Dad's. And Jerry says I have talent. He says I look like a young Tom Cruise. And he thinks my crooked smile will make people remember me.

I know I don't have much chance of being a big movie star. A lot of movie stars come to my house, and they're really awesome people. But I wouldn't mind maybe acting in some commercials and making a lot of money.

I started to toss stuff into my locker. But then I stopped and let out a groan. A brown envelope stuck out from the pile of books on the floor. My dad had asked me to mail it for him two days ago, but I forgot.

I'll mail it tomorrow, I decided. I slammed the locker shut and clicked the combination lock. I saw Cindy waving to me down the hall. But I shouted that I was late.

"Where are you going?" she called.

"Uh . . . got to help my mom do some charity work," I called back. "Collecting candles for the homeless!"

Why did I say that?

Why didn't I just tell her the truth? Sometimes I don't know why I make up these stories. I guess I do it because I can!

I flashed her a thumbs-up and made my way out the front door.

Dad's black Mercedes was parked right across the street. It was a sunny day, bright blue skies, hot as summer even though it was late autumn. The sun made the car sparkle like a big, black jewel.

"Yo yo yo!" Dad greeted me. "What up, Ross? What up, dude?" He thinks it's funny to talk really dumb, ancient rap talk. Mom says if we just ignore it, maybe he'll stop.

"Hi, Dad," I said. I slid onto the black leather passenger seat. "Ow." It was burning hot from the sun.

Dad checked himself out in the rearview mirror. He patted down the sides of his hair.

Dad is very young looking, and he's proud of it. He has straight brown hair and dark gray eyes, just like me. I see him check out his hair every time he passes a mirror, making sure he isn't losing any.

He's always tanned. He says it's part of the job. He always wears the same thing—black pants and a black T-shirt under an open sports jacket. He says it's the company uniform. Just like the black Mercedes is the company car.

Dad is always making fun of the movie business. But I know he loves being a studio big shot.

He checked the mirror again, then pulled the car away from the curb. I leaned forward and turned the air-conditioning to high.

"I've got to stop at the Universe Films lot and see a producer I'm trying to sign up," Dad said. "Then I'll take you to Jerry. How are you and Jerry getting along? Is he teaching you anything?"

"Yeah," I said. "It's good. We've mainly been reading scripts. You know. Out loud."

Dad snickered. "You ready for your screen test?"

I laughed, too. "Not yet."

The car phone rang. He pressed the phone button on the steering wheel and talked to his secretary about some budget mixups.

Palm trees rolled past us on both sides. Dad turned to me. "You mailed that envelope, right? It had very important contracts inside."

"Yeah. I mailed it," I said. A white lie. I knew I'd mail it tomorrow.

"Whew. That's good." Dad sighed. "If it's late, they'll nail my hide to the wall."

"No problem," I replied.

"I've been out of the 'hood, on location so long, we haven't had a chance to rap much," Dad said. "How's school?"

"Great!" I told him. "Miss Douglas said today I'll probably make the honor roll."

"Hey—all right!" Dad slapped me a high five and nearly drove off the road.

The phone rang again. Dad talked until we pulled into the Universe lot. The guard waved us through.

I'd been here with him before. We drove past the long, low white buildings until Dad found a parking space.

He ushered me into a big room that looked more like a living room than an office. It had two long, red leather couches, facing each other on a thick, white pile carpet, red drapes that matched the couches, three TV sets, a black-and-chrome bar, and bookshelves all around.

No desk.

"This is Mort's office," Dad said. "You wait here. I'll only be five minutes. This is really important to me. I've got to sign Mort on the dotted line."

He gestured to the tall shelves cluttered with framed photos, award statues, plaques, vases, and other junk. "Look around. But be careful, Ross. Don't touch anything. Mort is a nut about his collections. He goes berserk if he finds a fingerprint on anything!"

"No problem," I said.

"I've got to get this guy on my side," Dad said. Then he vanished out the door.

I settled onto one of the red couches. I sank

about two feet into the cushion! It was the softest couch I'd ever sat on in my life!

After a minute or two I got bored. I walked over to the shelves and began to check out all of the photos and awards.

I saw a framed photo of Mort and the President of the United States, grinning together on a golf course. It was signed by the President.

And there were dozens of other photos of Mort with movie stars and important-looking people.

One shelf held a knight's helmet and a gleaming silver sword. Probably props from a movie.

The next shelf was filled with award statuettes and plaques. I stopped in front of a familiar gold statue. An Academy Award! An Oscar!

I rubbed my hand over its smooth, shiny head. I realized I'd never touched an Oscar before.

"Totally cool!" I said out loud.

I couldn't stop myself. I had to hold it. I had to see how heavy it was, and what it felt like to actually hold an Oscar in my hand.

It was a lot heavier than I thought. I gripped it tightly in both hands. It was so smooth. The gold gleamed under the ceiling lights.

Holding it around the middle, I raised it high over my head. "Thank you!" I shouted to an imaginary audience. "Thank you for this award! I love it and I really deserve it!"

I raised the statuette higher—

—and it slipped from my hand.

I fumbled for it. Made a wild stab.

Missed.

And watched it crash to the floor.

It made such a heavy thud as it landed on its side. And then a horrible craaaack! I knew I'd never forget that sick sound.

I dropped to my knees to pick it up.

"Please be okay. . . . Please be okay!"

No. It wasn't okay.

The Oscar's round head had broken off.

I held the statue's body in one hand, the head in the other.

And then, still on my knees, I heard the rapid click of footsteps.

Someone was stepping into the office!

I froze in panic. My heart raced in my chest. I could hear the rasp of my rapid breaths.

I dived to the couch and frantically stuffed the Oscar—both pieces of it—under the couch.

I glanced up to see Dad enter the room. "Ross? What are you doing down on the floor?"

"Oh. I . . . dropped my chewing gum," I said. "But I got it back." I climbed shakily to my feet.

Dad eyed me curiously. "I thought I heard a crash in here. Is everything okay?"

I shrugged. "A crash? I didn't hear anything."

He studied me for a long moment. "Well . . . what did you do with the chewing gum?"

"Swallowed it," I said.

That struck him as funny. He laughed. "It went great with Mort. I think I won him over. Come on. Let's get you to Jerry's. You're late."

My knees were still shaking as we walked to the car. That was such a close one, I thought. But I should be okay now.

Of course, I was wrong.

We got home just before dinnertime. Hannah, our cook, was already bringing dishes to the table. Dad went into the den to make some phone calls.

I dropped my backpack in my room. Then turned to see my eight-year-old brother, Jake, walk in. "Hey—Jake the Snake!" I greeted him. I raised my hand. "Give me six!"

"I don't have six fingers!" Jake whined. "And stop calling me that!"

"Okay. How about Jake the Jerk?"

"Don't call me that, either!" My little brother is the Whining King of Beverly Hills.

You've probably already guessed that we don't get along. The problem is, Jake and I just don't have anything in common. He doesn't have a sense of humor. He isn't fast thinking.

He doesn't even look like me. He looks like Mom's side of the family—curly, carrot-colored hair, pale white skin, green eyes, a narrow rat face with his front teeth poking out.

"Hey, Rat Face!" I said. "What are you doing in my room?"

"I want my comic books back," he whined. Jake has a huge collection of Japanese comic books.

"Comic books? I don't read comic books," I said.

"You borrowed them!" Jake cried. "You borrowed them last week. You said you'd return them!"

"I never borrowed any comic books. Get lost," I said.

Why do I torture Jake like that? I don't know. I had the comic books in my bottom desk drawer. I could just hand them back to him. But I wanted to make him work for them.

He deserves it. He's such a whiner. And he never helps me out.

Last week I wanted to go hang out with some guys at the Planet Hollywood over on Wilshire. I begged Jake to tell Mom and Dad that I went to Sharma's house to study chemistry.

But he wouldn't do it. "I can't tell a lie!" he said.

"Why not?" I asked him.

"Because it's not right."

That's why I enjoy torturing him.

"I know where the comics are," he said. He dived past me and pulled open the bottom desk drawer. "There!"

I started to protest when I heard Dad's voice from downstairs. "Ross—get down here!"

Uh-oh. He sounded angry. Really angry.

I picked up the stack of comics and heaved them at Jake. Then I slowly made my way downstairs. "You called me?" I asked in a tiny voice.

Dad had his cell phone gripped tightly in one hand. "I have Mort on the phone," he said, scowling at me. "Mort says he changed his mind about working with me. He found the broken Oscar."

My mouth dropped open. "Oscar? What Oscar?"

"Ross, I told you not to touch anything. I told you

what a nut Mort is about his stuff. He found the Oscar pieces shoved under the couch."

"But . . . I sat on the couch the whole time," I said, my heart leaping around in my chest, my mouth suddenly dry. "I never saw any Oscar."

Dad said something into the phone, then clicked it off. He glared angrily at me. "You were the only one in the office."

"No," I replied. "Actually, a cleaning lady came in. Uh . . . two cleaning ladies, and I saw them dusting the shelves. I—"

Mom came in, carrying a load of shopping bags. "What's going on?"

"Ross is standing here, dissing me. He's lying to my face," Dad said, shaking his head. "Lying to my face!"

Mom sighed and let the bags drop to the carpet. "Ross," she whispered. "You're making up stories again?"

"No—" I started.

"Punish him!" Jake cried from the top of the stairs. "Punish him!"

"This is serious, Ross," Dad said, rolling the cell phone in his hand. "Very serious. You may have just lost me millions of dollars. You do have to be punished for this."

"Cut off his hand!" Jake shouted.

Mom gasped. "Jake! Where did you get a horrible idea like that?"

"It's what they do to liars," Jake said. "In some country somewhere. I learned it in school. Cut off his hand!"

Mom shook her head. "Well, we're not going to do that."

"No, we're not," Dad said. "We're going to do something much worse."

"You're grounded," Dad said.

He slapped the cell phone against his palm as if it was a policeman's club. "You've got to stop being so dishonest all the time."

"But I'm not!" I protested. "I—"

"You're grounded until I say you're not," Dad said sharply. Slap slap slap. The phone against his hand.

I swallowed hard. "But—what about Max's swim party Friday night? A lot of people are counting on me!" (Mainly the two girls I asked to go with me!)

"Sorry, Ross," Mom said softly. "You'll just have to miss it."

"But—I've learned my lesson!" I cried. "I'll never lie again. I swear!"

"He's lying." Jake walked into the room.

"Shut up!" I screamed at him. I turned back to Mom and Dad. "Really. I promise. I'll never tell another lie as long as I live."

"That's no good, Ross," Dad said firmly. "You have to prove yourself."

"I'll prove myself after Max's party," I said. "Please—?"

Mom and Dad both shook their heads. "No more arguing. You're grounded."

"Don't ground him. Cut off his hand!" Jake insisted.

Dad turned to Jake. "Jake, they cut off a hand for stealing—not for lying," Dad said.

"Oh," Jake replied. "Then cut off his lips!"

Mom and Dad burst out laughing.

I didn't think it was funny. With a growl I stomped up the stairs.

I deliberately bumped Jake into the wall. Swinging my fists, I raged into my room.

I was so furious, I thought I'd explode. "I hate my parents!" I screamed. And I kicked the wall with all my strength.

"Oh, wow."

My sneaker went right through the wall! Plaster crumbled to the floor. I had kicked a big hole in the wall!

"Ross? What was that?" Dad shouted.

"Uh . . . nothing," I called. "Nothing."

Friday night. Party night. And where was I?

In my brother's room, playing a stupid Nintendo wrestling game with Jake the Jerk.

Jake loves this game because it gives him a

chance to beat me up. On the screen, he pounds me and knocks me to the canvas. Then he jumps up and down on me for half an hour. Then he lifts me over his head and heaves me to the canvas a hundred times.

He goes nuts, furiously pushing the controller, beating me to a pulp.

It's a thrill for him.

But I wasn't thrilled. Stuck at home watching Jake while all my friends were partying. And Cindy and Sharma were there waiting for me, getting angrier and angrier.

Maybe I should have called them and told them I'd been grounded.

But I couldn't. It was too embarrassing.

Dad was thousands of miles away, in the Philippines, shooting a kung fu movie. Mom was visiting the Lamberts, friends of ours in Malibu.

The game ended. Jake pumped his fists above his head and did a victory dance.

Loud music floated in through the open window. Max's house was just down the block.

I leaned on the windowsill and peered out. I could see the lights from Max's pool. I heard kids shouting and laughing.

"I should be there," I muttered.

I turned to my brother. "Here's the deal," I said.

He shoved a game controller at me. "Come on. Let's go. Round Twelve."

"Here's the deal," I repeated. "I'm going to let you watch a DVD in my room."

That's usually a big deal to Jake. Because he doesn't have a DVD player in his room. And I have all the best movies.

But he frowned at me. "And where are you going?"

"Out," I said. "Just for a short while. Just for an hour. Then I'll be right back."

"I'll tell," Jake said.

I made a fist. "No, you won't."

"You're grounded, Ross," he said. "You're not allowed to go out. I'll tell."

"You can watch any movie you want," I said. "And you can eat a whole bag of M&M's. You don't have to share or save any for later."

A few minutes later I crept out of the house. I'd changed into a baggy, black swimsuit and a cool black-and-red Hawaiian shirt, my party shirt. And I packed a towel and a spare swimsuit into a plastic bag.

"Ross—!" Jake called from my bedroom window. "Ross—you'll be sorry!"

I just laughed.

"Party time!" I declared, taking my usual shortcut through the tall hedges, onto the terrace in Max's backyard. It was bright as day, and the teardrop-shaped pool sparkled. Dance music blasted from the big speakers on the roof of the pool house.

In the center of the terrace a man in a white jacket stood behind a table, making tacos. I glimpsed Max's parents sitting with some other adults away from everyone near the back of the house.

Wild splashing. Shouts. Loud laughter.

I saw a vicious splashing battle at one end of the pool. Some poor guy was being splashed by four or five girls, who were really into it.

Across from them a pool noodle war was taking place. Guys were smashing each other with pool noodles, beating each other, slapping backs and shoulders and heads. *Thwack. Thwaaack. Smaaaack.*

Two pool noodles cracked in half, and everyone laughed like crazy.

"Hey, Ross!" Max came hurrying over, carrying a

can of soda in one hand and a taco in the other.

Max is big. Big arms, big chest. He looks like a jock, but he isn't into sports at all.

He has short, spiky brown hair, and big brown eyes, and a grin that spreads over his entire face. And the girls all think he's one big puppy dog.

He was dripping wet. He'd just climbed out of the pool. He was wearing denim cutoffs, soaked to his skin. He had spilled some taco meat on his chest.

"Ross, I didn't think you were coming, man." He tried to flash me a thumbs-up and nearly dropped his taco.

"Hey, it's a party—right?" I replied. "So I'm here."

He chewed off a hunk of taco. "I heard you were grounded for life or something."

"No way!" I protested.

"That's what your brother said."

"He's crazy," I told Max. "Why would I be grounded?"

I saw Cindy jump up from a chair at the edge of the pool. She wore a white two-piece swimsuit. Her black hair bobbed behind her as she ran across the terrace toward me. "Hey, Ross—where were you?"

"Hi," I flashed her my best smile. "How's it going?"

"You're an hour late," she boomed, crossing her arms in front of her. "What happened?"

"Well . . ." I thought hard.

"It was my brother," I said. "Jake wasn't feeling

well. He was kind of sick. So I wanted to stay home and cheer him up. You know. Read him a few books. Play some games. I guess I lost track of the time."

Cindy's stern expression faded. "That was really nice of you," she said softly.

"Well, he's my only brother, you know. I try to take good care of him."

Over Cindy's shoulder, I saw Sharma waving frantically to me from the deep end of the pool.

"I'm starving," Cindy said. "Those tacos look really good. But I waited for you to get here." She started pulling me towards the food table.

"Uh . . . go get yourself one," I said. "I'll meet you over there in a sec. I just want to drop my bag somewhere."

She hurried to the taco guy, and I jogged around the pool to Sharma. "Hey—what's up?"

She narrowed her eyes at me. "Where have you been?"

I told her the same story about staying home to cheer up my brother. She ate it up, too.

"What were you talking to Cindy about?" she asked.

A Frisbee came flying out of the pool. I grabbed it and tossed it back. "Oh. Just something about school," I said.

"Want to get some tacos?" Sharma asked.

I looked across the pool and saw Cindy waiting for me by the taco table.

"Uh . . . not right now," I told Sharma. "I really need a swim. That water looks awesome, doesn't it? Why don't you get in, and I'll meet you in a sec?"

I spun away and hurried back to Cindy.

I'm going to be running back and forth between the two girls all night, I realized. This is like a totally bad TV sitcom. Only, it's my life!

"Here. I got you a taco," Cindy said, handing it to me. "What were you talking to Sharma about?"

"Just a school thing," I said. "She had a question about some homework."

Cindy stared at me suspiciously.

I turned and saw Sharma waving to me from the deep end of the pool.

How long did it take Cindy and Sharma to figure out the truth?

Not long.

Somehow, a few minutes later, all three of us found ourselves standing together at the edge of the pool. Cindy looked at Sharma. Sharma looked at Cindy.

"Are you here with Ross?" Cindy asked.

"Yes," Sharma replied. "You, too?"

"I can explain," I said.

They didn't give me a chance.

Cindy grabbed me around the waist. Sharma grabbed my legs. They picked me up—and heaved me into the pool.

I splashed hard.

The cold, clear water rose around me.

I bobbed to the surface. And felt hands grab my hair. And shove me back down.

"Hey—help!" I sputtered.

But they pushed me underwater. Held my head down.

I wrestled and thrashed my arms. I burst free. Shot up to the top, gasping and choking.

I saw them both laughing, both excited. They thought it was so funny.

They shoved me under again. And held me down.

I squirmed and kicked. But I couldn't pull free.

I could hear them laughing above me. They were paying me back. Having their revenge. Enjoying it so much.

They pushed my shoulders down. Pressed down on my head.

Too long . . . I thought. Too long!

I felt panic tighten my chest. I swallowed some water and started to choke.

Hey—I'm drowning! I realized.

Let me up! Too long! You're DROWNING me!

My chest ached. I swallowed more water.

Didn't they realize what they were doing?

Not funny! You're DROWNING me!

Lights flashed in the water. Blue. White. Blue. White.

I . . . can't . . . breathe . . .

And then—finally—I broke free.

The hands lifted. The weight vanished.

I shot up hard. And broke the surface, coughing and sputtering.

I sucked in breath after breath, my chest still aching. The lights flashed in my eyes.

The pool sparkled so brightly. . . . So painfully bright.

I shut my eyes and plunged back into the water.

I dived underwater and started to swim away from the two girls. Moving smoothly now, taking slow, steady strokes. I opened my eyes and swam, feeling my body start to relax.

I was nearing the deep end when I saw the figure

swimming toward me.

He was underwater, too, and taking the same slow strokes. He stared through the clear water at me.

At first I thought I was gazing at my reflection.

Did Max's parents put a mirror in the pool?

But no.

I was staring at another boy. Another boy swimming straight at me. A boy with my hair, my eyes, my face.

Closer . . .

The water was so clear . . . so bright and clear.

I stopped my swim strokes. I let my arms float to my sides. And I stared through the water . . . stared at a boy who looked exactly like me!

We both stopped and stared wide-eyed at each other. Lights shimmered and flashed in the water, making it seem unreal, like in a dream.

He seemed to be just as surprised to see me!

This isn't happening, I thought. He's a total twin. He's even wearing a baggy black swimsuit.

No. No way.

I swam closer.

His eyes grew wider. His expression changed. Now he looked angry. Upset.

Air bubbled from his open mouth.

And then he formed two words with his lips.

What was he saying? I struggled to understand.

Floating in place, I stared harder.

Go away.

That's what I thought he was saying.

More air bubbles escaped his open mouth, and he formed the words again:

Go away.

Why was he saying that? Why did he appear so angry?

Who was he? What was he doing here? I wanted to ask a dozen questions.

But my chest felt about to burst again.

I had to get air, had to breathe.

I raised my arms and kicked, and pulled myself up to the surface. Again, I took in breath after breath.

And then I waited for the other boy to surface.

He had to breathe, too—right?

I treaded water and waited, brushing water from my eyes, sweeping back my dark hair with one hand.

Where was he?

He didn't surface.

I swam slowly in his direction, my eyes searching the water.

I did a breast stroke, moving a few inches at a time, ducking my head under the surface, peering into the shimmering, blue light.

No.

No sign of him.

I reached the wall at the deep end, turned and floated back. I dived under, down to the pool floor, then back up to the top.

He was gone. Vanished.

But—how?

Who was he? Why did he look so much like me? Why did he tell me to go away?

Questions, questions.

I climbed out of the pool. Shook myself like a dog trying to get dry. I grabbed my towel and wrapped it around my shoulders.

Cindy and Sharma were still at the edge of the pool. They were laughing and dancing to the music blasting from the pool house.

I ran to them, waving frantically, my bare feet slapping the stone terrace. "Did you see that guy?"

They didn't stop dancing.

"Did you see him? The boy in the pool who looks like me?" I asked.

They ignored me. I guess they were still angry.

"I—I think I have a twin," I said.

Sharma scowled at me and rolled her eyes. "One of you is enough," she snapped.

"You really didn't see him?" I asked.

They kept dancing.

I suddenly realized it was getting late. "What time is it?" I asked.

They talked to each other as they danced and pretended I didn't exist.

I ran across the terrace to Max. He was kidding around with three girls from our class.

I slapped him on the back with a wet towel to get his attention.

"Got to run," I said. "I have to pick Jake up at a friend's house. Awesome party!"

"It's just starting!" he protested.

But I gave him a thumbs-up and took off. I stopped at the hedge and turned back.

Shielding my eyes from the bright lights, I

31

searched for the boy who looked so much like me.

No sign of him.

Cindy and Sharma were laughing hard about something. A boy did a bellyflop into the pool, sending up a high wave that drenched both of them.

I ducked through the crack in the hedge and began to jog across backyards toward my house. I knew I had to get home before Mom returned.

Jake the Snake would never lie for me. He'd love it if Mom got home first so he could tell her I sneaked off to Max's party.

I stopped at the bottom of the driveway and gazed up at the house. "Oh no," I moaned.

The lights were on in the front rooms. Mom's Jaguar was in the driveway.

No. No. No.

When did she get home? I wondered. Does she know that I'm not there?

Has Jake already squealed on me?

Keeping in the shadows, I made my way around to the side of the house.

The gardener planted a row of olive trees there a few years ago. The trees are short, but one of them is tall enough for me to stand on a branch and reach my bedroom window.

I only use it for emergencies.

And this was definitely an emergency.

If Mom found out that I left Jake by himself and sneaked out to Max's party, I'd be grounded until I was at least sixty years old!

I had to climb through the upstairs window into my bedroom, then walk downstairs as if I had been there all along.

If Jake said I went out, I'd tell Mom he was crazy.

I stopped a few feet from the olive tree. I gazed up at my dark bedroom window.

An easy climb.

No problem.

I reached for the bottom tree limb. Started to hoist myself up.

And two hands wrapped around my waist, grabbed me hard, and pulled me down.

As I fell back, I heard a high-pitched giggle in my ear.

I tumbled to the ground. Spun around quickly. Jumped to my feet.

And stared angrily at Jake.

"What are you doing out here?" I cried. My voice cracked.

That made Jake giggle even harder. His eyes flashed excitedly in the dim light. He loves scaring me. It's a total thrill for him to sneak up behind me and grab me or shout, "Boo!"

"What are you doing outside?" I repeated, grabbing him by the shoulders.

His grin grew wider. "I saw you coming."

I squeezed his tiny shoulders harder. "When did Mom get home? Does she know I went out?"

"Maybe," he replied. "Maybe I told her. Or maybe I didn't."

"Which is it?" I demanded.

"Maybe you have to find out," he said.

I loosened my grip. I smoothed the front of his T-shirt. "Listen, Jake, help me out here. I—"

The dining room window slid open. Mom poked her head out. "There you are, Rosssss."

I could tell by the way she hissed my name that she was totally angry.

"Get in here," she said. "Both of you. Right now." She slammed the window so hard, the glass panes shook.

She was waiting for us in the kitchen, hands pressed tightly against her waist. "Where were you, Rosssss?"

"Uh . . . nowhere," I said.

"You were nowhere?"

"Yeah," I said.

Jake laughed.

Mom's eyes burned into mine. "You weren't home when I got here. Were you?"

"Well . . . it's not what you're thinking," I said. "I mean, I didn't go to Max's party."

"Yes, you did!" Jake chimed in.

"Then where did you go?" Mom asked. "Why are you wearing a bathing suit? And why is it wet?"

"Uh . . . You see, Jake was watching a video. And I was so hot . . . I just went outside to cool off. I took a swim in our pool. Really. I knew I was grounded. So I just hung around the pool."

Jake laughed.

"Shut up, Jake!" I shouted. I spun away from

him. "He just wants to get me in trouble, Mom. I was in the backyard. Really."

Mom scrunched up her face as she studied me. I could tell she was trying to decide whether or not to believe me.

The phone rang.

Mom punched the button on the speakerphone. "Hello?"

"Oh, hi. Mrs. Arthur?"

I recognized Max's voice. I could hear the party going on in the background.

"Yes, Max. Did you want to speak to Ross?"

"No," Max replied. "I was just calling to tell him he left his towel and his extra suit at my house."

I slumped onto a kitchen stool. Caught again.

Mom thanked Max and clicked off the speakerphone. When she turned back to me, she did not have her friendly face on. In fact, she was bright red.

"I'm really worried about you, Ross," she said in a whisper.

"Huh? Worried?"

"I don't think you know how to tell the truth anymore."

"Sure, I do," I said. "I just—"

Mom shook her head. "No. Really, Ross. I don't think you know the difference between the truth and a lie."

I jumped off the stool. "I can tell the truth!" I protested. "I swear I can. Sometimes I make up things because . . . because I don't want to get in trouble."

"Ross, I don't think you can stop making up things," Mom said softly. "When your father gets back from his shoot, we need to have a family meeting. We need to talk about this problem."

I stared at the floor. "Okay," I replied.

And then I suddenly remembered the boy in the pool. And I had to ask.

"Mom, can I ask you a strange question? Do I have a twin?"

She narrowed her eyes at me for a long moment. Then her answer totally shocked me. "Yes," she said. "Yes, you do."

I gasped. "Huh?"

Mom nodded. "There's a good twin and a bad twin. You're the bad twin." She laughed.

"Ha ha," I said, rolling my eyes. "Good joke, Mom."

Mom squeezed my shoulder. "Why would I want two of you?"

"I want a twin!" Jake cried. "Then we could both pound Ross!"

"We have more serious problems to talk about," Mom said, sighing. "Let's drop the twin talk." She opened the refrigerator and pulled out a bottle of water. She raised it to her mouth and took a long drink.

"But I saw a kid who looks just like me," I said. "I mean, exactly like me. He could have been my twin!"

Mom took another drink, then shoved the bottle back into the fridge. "Were you looking in a mirror?"

I rolled my eyes again. "Ha ha. Another good one, Mom. Remind me to laugh later."

"I'm going to bed," Mom said. She clicked off the kitchen lights and started out of the room.

"No, wait." I hurried after her. "I really did see my twin."

As Mom turned back, she looked troubled and sad. "Ross, what am I going to do with you?" she whispered. "You really can't go two minutes without making up a story."

I felt my anger rise. I balled my hands into tight fists at my sides. "I'm not making this up," I screamed. "It's the truth!"

I pushed Jake out of the way and ran up to my room.

I couldn't get to sleep that night. I kept thinking about that boy swimming toward me in Max's pool. I kept picturing the angry expression on his face. I kept seeing him mouth the words *Go away*.

And then he vanished.

And I kept thinking about Cindy and Sharma. How angry they were over a simple mix-up.

Mom's words kept repeating in my mind: "I don't think you know the difference between the truth and a lie."

That was crazy. Totally wrong.

But how could I prove it to her?

Finally I drifted into a restless sleep. I dreamed that I was running through an endless field of tall grass, being chased by Cindy and Sharma. They were waving their arms furiously, calling to me, shouting their lungs out—but I couldn't hear them. And I couldn't stop running through the tall grass.

I was awakened by voices.

I sat straight up in bed, breathing hard. My pajama shirt clung wetly to my skin.

I glanced at my clock radio. Two o'clock in the morning.

Who was talking at this time of night? I held my breath and listened hard.

The voices came from downstairs. I heard a woman's voice. She was speaking loudly, sharply. But I couldn't make out her words.

Had Dad come home early from his shoot? Were he and Mom talking down there?

I slid out of bed and tiptoed to the hall. Nearly to the stairs, I stopped and listened again.

It was dark downstairs. No lights on in the living room. They must be in the kitchen, I realized.

The woman was talking. It was Mom. I recognized her voice.

I leaned into the stairwell to try to make out her words.

"Are you going crazy or something?"

That's what she said. She didn't sound angry. She sounded worried.

"You don't have a twin," she said. "No twin. Why would you say such a crazy thing?"

And then I heard a boy answer.

"But I saw him!" the boy said. "Really. I saw him."

I let out a low gasp. I gripped the banister to keep from falling.

The boy . . .

The boy . . . had MY voice!

"I'm not making it up," the boy said—in my voice. "I saw him, and he saw me."

"It's late. We should be asleep," Mom said. "Come on. Turn off the lights."

"Why don't you believe me?" the boy demanded shrilly.

Gripping the banister, I realized my whole body was trembling.

How can he have my voice? Who is he? Why is Mom talking to him in the middle of the night?

I had to see what was going on. I took a step—and stumbled.

My bare foot slid over the wooden stair, and I started to fall, tumbling down step by step.

A painful thud with each step.

I landed hard on my elbows and knees. My heart pounding, I waited for the pain to stop. And listened for approaching footsteps, for cries of surprise from the kitchen.

Mom must have heard me thumping and

bumping down the stairs.

Why didn't she come running to see who had fallen?

Silence in the kitchen now.

I picked myself up and straightened my pajamas. One knee throbbed with pain. I rubbed it carefully as I limped toward the kitchen.

"Who's down here?" I called. "Mom? Is that you?"

No reply.

The kitchen was dark. No lights on. Silvery moonlight poured in from the windows. No color in the room, only shades of gray.

I suddenly felt as if I were in a black-and-white movie.

"Mom? I heard you talking!" I called.

I made my way across the kitchen, running my hand along the counter. "Anyone in here?"

No.

I peered out at the backyard. Under the bright moonlight, the swimming pool shimmered, and the grass glowed like silver.

Unreal.

I turned away—and the kitchen lights flashed on. Blinking from the shock of the light, I saw Mom in the doorway.

"Ross? What are you doing down here?" she asked, holding a hand over her mouth and yawning loudly.

"I—I heard you talking," I said.

She tightened the belt of her robe. "Me? It wasn't me. I was asleep."

"No," I said. "I heard voices. You were here in the kitchen, talking to a boy."

Mom rubbed her eyes with both hands. "No. Really, Ross. Why are you down here?"

"I told you," I said, clenching my fists. I banged one fist on the Formica counter. "Why don't you believe me?"

"Because I wasn't in here talking to anyone," Mom said. "I was in my bed, sound asleep. Until I heard you wandering around."

She yawned. "You must have been having a nightmare. Sometimes nightmares can seem very real."

"I didn't dream it," I insisted. "I know the difference between a nightmare and what's really happening."

I could see she wasn't going to believe me. So I shrugged and followed her out of the kitchen, clicking off the lights as I left.

I didn't get back to sleep that night.

I lay in bed, staring up at the ceiling. Listening for the voices downstairs. Waiting . . . listening for Mom and the boy with my voice.

I didn't know I would see the boy in a few hours.

I didn't know how dangerous he was.

I didn't know the terrifying trouble I was in.

Cindy stopped me after school Monday afternoon. I was kneeling down in front of my hall locker, lacing my new tennis sneakers. She stepped in front of me and stomped down hard on one of them.

"Hey!" I snapped angrily. "Why'd you do that?"

She shrugged. "Just felt like it."

I tied the laces quickly, then spit on my fingers and tried to rub off the scuff mark she'd made. "If you're still angry at me about Max's party . . ."

"I've decided to be nice to you again," she said.

"Nice? By stomping on my foot?"

She laughed. "That was just to be funny." She raked her fingers through her straight black bangs. "Why did you leave the party so early Friday night? Afraid Sharma and I would toss you in the pool again?"

"You almost drowned me!" I grumbled.

"You deserved it," Cindy replied. "So why did you leave in such a hurry, Ross?"

"Oh, I was worried about my little brother," I said.

"I don't like to leave him alone for long."

Cindy stared hard at me. "Is that the truth?"

I slammed my locker shut. "Of course," I said.

Cindy shifted her backpack on her shoulders. "Maybe you could come over to my house now. We could study for the government test together."

I waved to some guys down the hall. "I can't," I told Cindy. "I have tennis team practice."

I glanced at the clock above the principal's office. "I'm already late."

Cindy frowned at me. "Where's your tennis racket?"

I started jogging to the back doors. "Steve Franklin said he'd bring an extra one for me. I left mine at home this morning."

"Where are you really going?" Cindy called after me. "Why don't you tell me the truth?"

"It's true!" I shouted. I trotted out of the school building and hurried across the playground to the tennis courts.

I heard the *thock thock thock* of rackets hitting tennis balls. Guys on the team were already warming up.

I searched the long row of courts for Steve Franklin. He had a bucket of balls and was hitting one after another, practicing his serve.

I started jogging over to him to get the racket he'd promised to bring. But Coach Melvin blocked my way. "Ross, you're ten minutes late. We really need you here on time. You missed the whole warm-up."

"Sorry, Coach," I said. "I . . . uh . . . had a really bad nosebleed."

He squinted at my nose. "You okay now?"

I nodded.

"Well, go warm up. Practice your serves, okay? Take the court next to Steve."

I took a basket of tennis balls and trotted over to Steve. He stopped serving and tossed me an old racket of his. "What's up, Ross?" he asked.

I swung the racket hard a few times to get the feel of it.

"I'm thinking of quitting the team," I said. "I might go pro."

Steve laughed. "Yeah. Me, too."

"Not a bad racket," I said, twirling it in my palm. "Not a good racket. But not a bad racket."

"You want to come over and practice some time this weekend?" Steve asked. "My dad built a new court in our backyard. It's clay. Very sweet."

"Cool," I said. I dragged the bucket of balls over to the next court and started practicing my serve. The first three flew into the net.

I turned and saw Coach Melvin frowning at me from the next court.

"Just testing the racket," I called to him.

I served a few more. My arm felt stiff. I hadn't practiced in a while.

Down the long row of courts, guys were volleying back and forth. The afternoon sun suddenly appeared from behind a high cloud. The bright light swept over me.

I shielded my eyes with one hand—and saw him.

Squinting into the sunlight, I saw the boy—me!—my twin. He was six or seven courts down, at the far end.

He was volleying with Jared Harris. He was dressed in the same tennis whites I wore. His dark hair flew up as he ran to the net.

He looked just like me!

The racket fell out of my hand and bounced in front of me.

"Hey!" I shouted. I waved frantically.

He didn't hear me. He returned a serve from Jared, then ran to the corner to return Jared's shot.

"Hey—you!" I cried. "Wait!"

My heart pounded. I squinted hard, trying to block out the bright sunlight. Trying to make sure I wasn't seeing things.

No. It was me.

It was my exact double on that court.

And suddenly he turned—and saw me.

I saw his eyes go wide. I saw his expression change. He recognized me.

For a long moment we stared at each other down the long row of tennis courts.

And then his mouth formed the words . . . the same words they had formed underwater in Max's pool: *Go away.*

Even from so far away, I could see the angry scowl on his face. Cold . . . His glare was so cold.

"GO AWAY!" he repeated.

"No!" I screamed. "No!"

I started to run, shouting and waving my arms wildly.

I got about two steps and tripped over the racket I had dropped.

The racket slid under my feet. I fell onto my stomach and bounced hard over the asphalt.

"Owww!"

Ignoring the pain, I scrambled to my feet. Lurched a few steps toward the far court—and stopped.

The boy—my twin—was gone. Vanished again.

I stared into the light. Jared had his back turned. He was leaning over, pulling a white headband out of a canvas bag.

He had missed the whole thing!

Finally Jared turned around. "Hey, Ross," he called. "Are you going to play or not?"

I ran over to him. "Th-that wasn't me," I said.

He narrowed his eyes at me. "Excuse me? I thought we were playing a practice game."

"It wasn't me," I repeated shakily.

The guys in the next court had stopped playing. They were staring at me now.

I saw Coach Melvin jogging over from the other end of the courts.

"That boy—" I said to Jared. "Did he tell you his name or anything?"

Jared laughed. "I don't get the joke, Ross."

"It—it wasn't me!" I cried shrilly.

Jared shook his head. "Well, he looked like you, and he talked like you, and he sounded just like you. And he played like you. So . . ."

"What's the problem, Ross?" Coach Melvin hurried up to us, gazing at me sternly. "What's happening?"

"Uh . . . nothing," I said. "Really. Nothing."

I felt dazed. Kind of dizzy.

The bright sunlight turned white . . . white . . . whiter. It flashed in my eyes.

What's going on? I wondered.

Who *is* that kid?

"Sharma—hey!" I saw her on the steps in front of school and ran over to her. "You stayed after?"

She nodded. "I had a makeup test in government. It wasn't too bad."

"That means you aced it," I said. Sharma is a total brain, but she doesn't like kids to say it. Her idea of a bad test score is anything below 110!

"Are you walking home?" I asked. "Can I walk with you?"

She nodded again. She pulled a bug or something off my tennis shirt. "How was tennis practice?"

"Totally weird," I said. As we started to walk, I decided to tell her the whole story. I had to tell someone!

"This kid is my exact twin," I told her. "But he keeps disappearing before I can talk to him. Today, he was at tennis practice, playing with Jared. But it wasn't the first time I saw him. I saw him in Max's pool Friday night. He was swimming right at me!"

Sharma laughed. "You make up the dumbest stories."

"No. I'm serious!" I said. "He is my exact twin. In every way. He even wears the same clothes as me."

"Give me a break," Sharma said. "You should be a writer, Ross. You have such an awesome imagination."

I groaned. "But I'm not making it up. Why won't anyone believe me?"

"Because it's crazy?" Sharma suggested.

We stopped at a corner. "I'm telling the truth," I insisted. "I saw this boy twice. And he was me. Really."

Sharma narrowed her eyes at me. "Do you believe in ghosts?"

"Ghosts? No," I said. "Why?"

"Well, I saw this movie on TV about a girl who kept seeing her twin. And her twin turned out to be her ghost. The ghost came back from the future because she wanted to possess herself and take over her own life."

"That doesn't make any sense at all," I muttered.

"I know," Sharma said. "But maybe the boy you keep seeing is your own ghost."

"But don't I have to die to have a ghost?" I asked.

Traffic drowned out Sharma's answer. Cars whirred through the intersection. The afternoon sun was lowering behind the hills. People were speeding home from work.

The light turned green. I started to walk.

"Hey—stop!" Sharma pulled me back. "Where are you going?"

"But the light—" I protested.

"You're so busy making up invisible twins, you don't know what you're doing!" Sharma said.

"He's not invisible," I told her.

The light turned red. Sharma tugged me into the street. "We can go now."

"Huh? You're going to get us killed!" I cried.

I pulled back and stumbled over the curb. Sharma laughed as I fell flat on my back on the grass. "What is your problem, Ross? Have you totally lost it?"

I pulled myself up and brushed off the back of my jeans. "Sorry," I said. "But you started to walk on red, and—"

I realized she was staring over my shoulder. Not listening to me. She was waving at Cindy who was coming our way.

I glanced down—and uttered a cry of surprise.

The grass where I had fallen—it had turned brown. You could see the outline of my shoulders and my back and one of my arms.

The grass along the curb was all green—except for where my body had touched it.

And as I stared, the patch of brown grass made a sizzling sound, as if it was on fire. Black smoke floated up.

The grass burned away until the outline of my back and shoulders was bare dirt.

"Wow," I murmured. "That is so weird! Sharma—look at this."

I glanced up to see Sharma walking away. "See you, Ross." She gave me a quick wave. "I have to talk to Cindy."

"Wait, Sharma! Come back!" I shouted.

"We'll walk home together tomorrow, Ross. Hey, why don't you invite your ghost? We can all walk home together!" She laughed as she headed down the street to Cindy.

"Sharma! Hey—Sharma!" I called after her. But she didn't slow down or turn back.

I stared down at the grass again. "What is that about?" I muttered. I waited for the traffic to stop. Then I ran across the street and kept running until I reached home.

The gardeners were just finishing for the day, packing up their truck. I ran through the front lawn sprinklers. The cold water felt great!

To my surprise, Mom was waiting for me at the front door. "What's wrong?" I cried.

"Nothing is wrong," she said. "Your karate teacher just called. He said—"

"My what?" I interrupted.

"Mr. Lawrence said he's coming early. Right after dinner. So, if you have homework to do . . ."

"But—but—but—" I sputtered. "I don't take karate lessons, Mom!"

Her mouth dropped open. She narrowed her eyes at me. "Only since you were seven," she said.

I felt a chill run down my back.

She wasn't joking.

But how could she say that?

The only karate I ever did was in Nintendo games!

"Don't just stand there, Ross. Come in," Mom said. "How was your tennis practice?"

"Weird," I said. I opened my mouth to tell her about seeing my twin again. But I stopped myself. She'd just think I was making it up.

"Why was it weird?" she asked.

"Well . . . I played so well for a change. No one could touch my serve. Coach Melvin thinks I'm going to be the star player on the team this year."

"Excellent," Mom said. She hugged me. "We'll have an early dinner since your karate lesson is early. You can thank me in advance. I made your favorite."

"My favorite?"

"Yes. Brussels sprouts. Jake won't eat them. But I know you love them."

Huh? Brussels sprouts? I HATE them! Just thinking about them makes me want to puke!

"Mom?" I cried weakly. "What is going on here?"

She didn't hear my question. The phone rang, and she hurried to answer it.

I was going to ask where Jake was. But then I remembered that he has his guitar lesson on Mondays. Amelia, our housekeeper, always brings him home around dinnertime.

I made my way up to my room to change out of my tennis whites. I opened my closet door—and gasped.

A white karate robe hung on the door hook.

How did that get here? I wondered.

I backed out of the closet and glanced quickly around my room. Had anything else changed? Was I into other activities that I had no memory of?

My eyes swept over my Jimi Hendrix posters, my autographed baseballs, my snow globe collection, my stuffed leopard from when I was four.

Everything was there. Everything was the same.

Except for that white robe in my closet.

And the sour smell of brussels sprouts floating up

from the kitchen downstairs. How could Mom forget how much I hate brussels sprouts?

I started to change into a clean pair of baggy jeans and a black T-shirt. But as I pulled the shirt from my dresser drawer, a sharp pain shot through my forehead.

"Huh—?" I gasped. The shirt fell from my hands.

I grabbed my head as another pain rocked through it. I saw a white flash, like a lightning bolt. I pressed my hands tightly to my head.

"Ohhh . . . what is happening?"

Stab after stab of pain pierced my head. I felt as if someone kept jamming a knife into my eyes.

I dropped to my knees, weak from pain. Flash after flash of white light blinded me.

"Whoa . . ."

And then it stopped.

I blinked several times. Still holding my head, I waited for the pain to return.

But I felt normal again. I opened my eyes. I could see clearly.

Shaking my head, I climbed to my feet. What was that about? I'd never had a headache like that before.

I stared out the window, breathing slowly, trying to get my head straight—when Mom called me from downstairs. "Ross, I need you to do me a favor."

I pulled on the T-shirt, brushed back my hair. Then, still feeling shaky, I made my way down the stairs and met her at the bottom.

"I just had the worst headache," I groaned.

She rolled her eyes. "Ross, why do you always have a headache when I need you to do me a favor?"

"No. Really," I insisted. "But I'm okay now. What's the favor?"

"The milk went sour," she said, holding her nose. "I need you to go to the store and buy another carton."

My mouth dropped open. "Huh? Walk to the store? This is Beverly Hills, Mom. People don't walk to the store. That's too weird. Why don't you drive?"

"I can't," she said. "I'm waiting for a call from your dad. He's been so busy on the set, I haven't spoken to him in three days."

"But he can call you in the car," I said. "It's almost four blocks to the store, and—"

"Ross, just go," Mom said. She stuffed a twenty-dollar bill into my T-shirt pocket.

Normally, I'd come up with a great excuse: "I can't walk that far. I sprained my ankle at tennis practice. Coach Melvin said I should stay off my foot all week."

But I decided it would be good to get out of the house. It would give me time to think about all the weird stuff that was happening.

"Back in a few minutes," I said. I took off, walking fast.

I had walked about two blocks—halfway to the

store—when I saw my twin. He was half a block ahead of me, walking fast.

He was wearing baggy jeans and a black T-shirt, just like me. He had Walkman headphones over his ears and was snapping his fingers, jiving along.

I stopped in shock. My heart started to pound.

"This time you're not getting away!" I said out loud.

I took off, running full speed to catch up to him. He had the music blasting in his ears. So he didn't hear me.

You're not getting away. You're not getting away. I chanted those words in my mind as I ran.

I stretched out my arms as I caught up with him.

I grabbed him by the shoulders. He was real!

I grabbed him from behind. Spun him around.

And gasped in shock.

Not him! It wasn't my twin!

It was another guy, a stranger.

His dark eyes bulged in surprise. His mouth dropped open.

I held my grip on his shoulder. I was too startled to move.

And then I felt the shoulder move under my hand. It started to wriggle . . . then shrink . . . to melt away.

I uttered a cry. My hand flew off his shoulder.

And I stared in horror as the boy's shoulder shrank under the sleeve of the black T-shirt. And his hand . . . his hand clenched in a tight fist . . . grew smaller . . . melted away . . . melted into the wrist.

And then the arm curled like a fat snake. Boneless . . . No longer a human arm, it twisted and curled, and reached out for me like the tendril of a plant.

"You . . . You . . .You . . ." the boy choked out in a hoarse gasp.

"Huh?" I gasped. I stepped back, trying to escape the curling tendril of an arm.

He uttered a gurgling sound, tore off the headphones, and staggered toward me.

I slapped my hand over my mouth to keep from screaming as his face began to change.

The skin peeled away. Peeled off like onion skin . . . flaked away in chunks . . . until he had no skin.

No skin on his face at all!

His hair fell off in thick clumps. And then the pale skin flaked off his scalp. And now his whole head glowed bright red. Red and wet.

Just like raw meat.

His face was raw meat, chunks of meat, crisscrossed with bulging purple veins.

His dark eyes stared out at me from wet sockets.

No nose. Just two deep holes, two gaping nostrils carved into the meaty slab.

"The pain. It hurts," he moaned.

His whole face jiggled and throbbed.

I staggered back. "What—what's happening to you?" I stammered, raising my hands to shield myself from the hideous sight of his raw face. From his arm, wriggling in front of him like a pale snake.

He tossed back his throbbing, glistening red face and uttered a shrill howl.

And then he spun away—and took off, howling as he ran. And screaming at the top of his lungs, "Help! Help!"

I grabbed my stomach. I felt sick.

What just happened? I wondered, hugging myself, trying to stop trembling.

I shook my head to try to clear it.

But I couldn't force the picture of the kid's face from my mind. The throbbing red meat, glistening and wet. The purple veins pulsing in his choppy face.

"I've got to get away from here!" I said out loud. I started to jog—but another sharp pain shot through my head.

On fire, I thought. My head is on fire!

I grabbed my head with both hands. Stab after stab of pain made me cry out. I shut my eyes. I pressed my hands tighter over my throbbing head.

Once again the pain stopped as abruptly as it had started.

I shook my head hard. I saw the little grocery store up ahead. It'll be cool inside, I decided.

And normal.

Please, I pleaded silently, let everything be normal again.

The store was nearly empty. A couple of teenagers were discussing candy bars at the front counter. A boy was trying to get his friend to buy a Zigfruit bar. His friend said only freaks buy Zigfruits. He was sticking with Four Musketeers.

Zigfruits? Four Musketeers?

Since when did they add another musketeer?

I picked a carton of milk off the shelf and carried it to the woman behind the counter. "Is that all?" she asked.

I nodded. "Yes. Just the milk."

I shoved the carton across the counter.

And felt the cardboard carton melt away in my hand.

The milk poured out, steaming . . . making a loud hissing sound.

"Oh!" I gasped as the hissing milk poured out in thick lumps. It spread over the counter. Bubbling . . . steaming . . . turning bright yellow.

A sick, sour smell rose up from the yellow clots.

The shocked woman gazed down at the steaming mess. Then raised her eyes to me—frightened eyes—and opened her mouth in a scream: "GET OUT! OUT! GET OUT OF HERE!"

"S-sorry!" I choked out. My stomach lurched from the sick smell. I gagged. Spun away from the counter—and staggered outside.

I stumbled to the curb, feeling dazed, sick. I glimpsed the two guys from the store, holding strange candy bars, staring at me from the doorway.

"Hey—!" I called to them. My legs shaking, my whole body trembling, I walked up to them. "What just happened?" I asked. "Did you see—?"

"Don't touch us!" one of them screamed.

They both raised their hands as if shielding

themselves from me.

"Keep back! Don't touch us!"

"But—but—" I sputtered. "What's wrong? What's happening?"

The two boys scrambled away. One of them dropped his candy bar. He didn't stop to pick it up.

I ran all the way home. Gasping for breath, sweat pouring down my face, I burst into the house.

"Mom? Where are you? Mom?"

"In the dining room," she called. "Jake and I started without you."

I lurched into the dining room. Mom and Jake sat at one end of the long table. Jake opened his mouth wide and showed me a disgusting, chewed-up blob of spaghetti inside.

I ran up beside Mom's chair. "I—I have to talk to you," I said.

"Sit down," Mom said sharply. "What took you so long? Mr. Lawrence will be here any minute."

"Listen to me!" I cried. "Something strange is going on and—"

"Your face is strange!" Jake shouted. He burst out laughing at his own dumb joke.

"At least my nickname isn't Rat Face!" I shot

back. "Hi, Rat Face! What's up, Rat Face!"

"I'm not a Rat Face! You're a rat! You're a whole rat!" Jake screamed. "Go eat some cheese, Rat!"

"Stop it! Stop it right now!" Mom cried. She turned to me. "Where's the milk?"

"That's what I'm trying to tell you," I said breathlessly. "I couldn't—"

"You came home without milk?" Mom sighed. "Sit down, Ross." She pushed me toward my seat. "Don't talk. Try to eat something before your lesson."

"But—But—"

"Don't talk! Just eat!" She scooped a mound of spaghetti onto my plate. Then she piled on a ton of brussels sprouts.

Yuck.

The smell made my stomach lurch.

Mom leaned over the table, watching me. "Go ahead. Try the sprouts. I know you love them."

"We have to talk—" I started. "You see, I don't like brussels sprouts. I'm trying to tell you—"

She shook her head. "Stop it. Not a word. I've heard enough of your crazy stories to last a lifetime. Just eat."

I had no choice. I speared one of the disgusting, squishy balls on my fork. I raised it slowly to my mouth.

I felt sick. My stomach tightened.

I started to gag.

Mom stared across the table at me.

I held my breath. And slid the brussels sprout into my mouth. So squishy and slimy and sour . . .

I swallowed it whole.

Mom sat back in her seat. "Good?"

I couldn't reply. I was trying with all my strength to keep from puking.

The front doorbell rang. I saw Amelia, the house-keeper, hurry to answer it.

"That's Mr. Lawrence," Mom said. "Hurry, Ross. Get into your karate robe. You'll have to eat later. We'll keep dinner warm for you."

I gulped down a glass of apple juice, trying to get the brussels sprouts taste out of my mouth. "Uh . . . maybe I should skip the lesson tonight," I said. "I have a big homework project, and—"

"Mr. Lawrence drove all the way from Burbank," Mom said. "Get upstairs and get changed. What's wrong with you tonight?"

That's what I want to know! I said to myself as I hurried to my room.

What's wrong with me tonight?

I stared at the white robe hanging on my closet door. Which way does the belt go? I wondered. Does the collar stay up or down?

How am I going to fake my way through this lesson? I asked myself. I can't. I don't know any-thing about karate. And I've never seen this Mr. Lawrence before in my life.

Why did Mom say I've been taking lessons since I was seven?

How can she be so totally confused?

I pulled on the robe and tied the belt in front of me. My hands were trembling.

This guy could kill me, I realized.

I can't go through with this. I've got to stop it.

Downstairs, I heard voices coming from Dad's gym in the back of the house. Dad has a Stairmaster, a weight bench, and a treadmill in there.

As I stepped into the room, I was surprised to see a canvas floor mat spread out in the center of the gym. Jake was on the mat, kidding around with a huge, bald, red-faced man in a white robe. Mr. Lawrence.

The karate teacher was letting Jake throw him over his little shoulder. Jake laughed as Mr. Lawrence flipped over and landed with a hard thud on his back.

"You didn't know you were so strong, did you?" Mr. Lawrence asked Jake.

"I'm stronger than Ross!" Jake bragged. He crooked both arms to show off his pitiful, pea-sized muscles.

Mr. Lawrence sprang easily to his feet and turned to me. "Hi, Ross. You ready?" He bowed to me.

I bowed back. "Uh . . . I don't think I can do this tonight," I started. "You see, I've had these terrible headaches—"

"Tension," Mr. Lawrence said. "This lesson should help."

"No. Really," I insisted. "Maybe . . . uh . . . Jake would like a lesson tonight. I can't—"

He wasn't paying any attention to me. "Let's practice what we were doing last time, okay?"

He stood stiffly, facing me, hands placed firmly on his hips. He stared straight ahead, concentrating. His round, bald head glowed under the ceiling light.

What is he waiting for? I wondered. What is he going to do?

It didn't take long to find out.

With a grunt, he swung off the floor. Flew up off the mat. Both legs rose sideways—and landed a hard, pounding kick in my stomach.

"Unnnnh!" I groaned in pain.

I doubled over. It hurt . . . hurt so much . . . I couldn't breathe . . . couldn't breathe . . .

I felt my stomach tighten—then heave.

"Unnnnnh." The whole brussels sprout flew out of my mouth and plopped onto the mat.

Gasping, holding my aching stomach, I collapsed to the floor.

Mr. Lawrence huddled over me. "What happened?" He knelt beside me, his heavy arm on my shoulders. "Ross, you've defended against that a hundred times. Why didn't you move?"

"Uh . . ." I couldn't speak. My breaths were rasping in my throat.

Somehow I managed to stand. My stomach ached. I felt about to heave again.

"Ross, are you okay? Why didn't you defend yourself?" Mr. Lawrence asked.

I turned away. Bent over, I started to run. Out of the gym. Down the back hall.

"Ross, come back!" Mr. Lawrence shouted after me.

I was nearly to the stairs when a figure jumped out to stop me.

My twin.

I let out a startled cry. "You—?"

Scowling at me furiously, he grabbed my arm. "I'm late—and you try to take over my life! It's not going to work, Rosssss," he hissed. "Give me that robe—and get out of here!"

"But—" I groaned weakly.

"Get out! Go away!" he cried in a harsh whisper. "I've been warning you! You don't belong here!"

Angrily I pushed his hand away. "Get off me!" I cried.

"Go away, Rossss!" he hissed. He shoved me. "You don't belong here. You have to leave."

"But—it's my house!" I cried. "Who are you? What are you doing here?"

He raised a finger to his lips and glanced nervously down the hall. "Keep it down. I can't explain. But I'm trying to tell you—you're in danger. Don't say anything. Don't touch anything. Just give me that robe and get lost! Fast!"

"I won't leave!" I insisted. "You have to leave! I'm going to tell Mom. I'm going to explain that you aren't me!"

"She's *my* Mom!" my twin declared. "Please! Leave! Just—go!"

"No way!" I said.

I heard voices from the gym. Footsteps in the hall.

"Get upstairs!" my twin whispered frantically. He grabbed the robe and struggled to tug it off me. I let him take it. Then he pushed me to the stairs.

"What's going on?" I demanded. "Who are you? Why do you look like me?"

"I can't explain now. Go up to my room—quick!"

"It's my room!" I protested.

"Get upstairs before they see you!" he ordered.

"But I have to talk to Mom!" I said.

"No way." He twisted my arm up hard behind my back.

"Ow."

He's real, I realized. He's a person. He's not a ghost. A ghost couldn't shove me or twist my arm like that.

Squeezing my arm behind my back, he forced me up the stairs and into my room. "You can't—" I started to say.

But he practically heaved me into the room. "I'll come back after the lesson. I'll explain," he said breathlessly. "Don't try to escape. And don't touch anything. I'm warning you."

Then he hurried back out to the hall and closed the bedroom door behind him.

"No! Wait!" I shouted.

I grabbed the doorknob and started to pull the door open. But I heard the lock click on the other side.

He'd locked me in.

"Hey—come back!" I shouted. I pounded on the door with my fists. "Give me a break! Let me out of here!"

I pounded till my fists hurt. Silence out there.

With a defeated sigh, I slumped away from the door. I'm a prisoner, I realized. A prisoner in my own room.

But was it my room?

I spun around. My eyes swept over all the familiar things. My Jimi Hendrix posters . . . my snow globe collection . . . my things.

Yes. I was in my own room. My room in my house.

But why does everything seem right and wrong at the same time?

I remembered falling. Then watching the grass burn.

I thought about the boy on the street. I had grabbed his shoulder, and his arm had changed until it slithered and curled. And his face . . .

I didn't want to think about that hamburger face.

The milk in the store. I held the carton . . . and it blew up or something! And then everyone started screaming at me.

What was going on?

Did I cause those things to happen?

Why? How could I?

I paced back and forth, my heart pounding. I clenched and unclenched my fists. I stopped at the window and peered out.

A warm, clear night. Stars in a purple sky. The olive tree below the window shimmered in a soft wind, as if inviting me. Inviting me to climb out and lower myself down its trunk.

Yes!

I'll escape, I decided. Then I'll run back inside the house and find Mom. I'll show her the other Ross. I'll tell her he's an impostor, a total fake. I'll make her believe me. And I'll tell her about all the other weird things that have happened. There's got to be a logical explanation for all of it. Once Mom sees the other Ross, she'll know I'm not lying. She'll help me figure out what's going on.

My hands trembled as I reached for the window. I slid it up as high as it would go. Warm, damp air floated into the room. It smelled so sweet and fresh.

I lowered myself onto the windowsill and slid one leg over the side.

This was the tricky part. The nearest branch was a foot or two below the window. I had to lower my feet onto it carefully, then swing my body out and grab onto the slender trunk.

If I slipped . . .

I didn't want to think about it.

I turned and started to swing my other leg out the window.

But I stopped when I saw the bedroom door open behind me. My twin burst in, still wearing his karate robe. His eyes searched the room, then stopped when he spotted me at the window.

"Good!" he said. "Go. You have to go. There isn't room for both of us!"

And then I gasped as he dived forward, arms outstretched. Running to push me out the window.

I spun to fight him off.

But my leg caught on the side of the house.

He grabbed my arm with both hands. And to my shock, pulled me back into the room.

I landed on the floor, breathing hard, my body bathed in a cold sweat.

He stared down at me, a crooked smile on his face. My crooked smile.

"Did you think I was going to push you out?" he asked, breathing hard.

"Well . . . maybe," I muttered.

I climbed slowly to my feet. I stood facing him, tensed and ready.

"I'd love to push you out," he said, squinting at me angrily. "But the fall wouldn't kill you. And I have to get you out of here—out of here for good."

"So why didn't you let me go out the window?" I demanded.

"You wouldn't get very far," he said menacingly.

"What do you mean?" I demanded.

"You don't understand. You don't know anything," my twin said, shaking his head. "I guess I have no choice. I have to explain it all before you go."

"But I'm not going," I said firmly, crossing my arms in front of me. "You are going. You are the one who doesn't belong."

He made a disgusted face and motioned for me to sit down.

I dropped down tensely on the edge of the bed. He tugged off the white robe and tossed it into the closet. Then he pulled out the desk chair and sat on it backward, resting his hands on its back.

"This is your own fault," he said bitterly. He glanced to the door. I guessed he was making sure it was closed.

"My own fault?" I cried. "What are you talking about?"

"You told a lot of lies—didn't you!" he accused. "You lied and lied and lied. You told so many lies, you broke the fabric of truth and reality!"

"I didn't lie that much!" I protested.

"Ross, you lied so much, you lost all track of what's real and what isn't real," he continued. "You slipped into a parallel world. Into a whole different reality. Out of your world—into my world."

I jumped to my feet. "Are you crazy?" I shouted. "What are you talking about?"

"Didn't you learn about parallel worlds?" my twin asked. "What kind of school do you go to? We study that in fourth grade."

"You're totally crazy," I muttered, dropping back onto the bed.

"Well, didn't you notice things are a little different here?" my twin demanded. "Didn't you notice that things are almost the same—but not quite?"

"Well . . . yeah," I replied.

My twin climbed to his feet. He shoved the chair back under the desk. "You lied and lied until you lost your reality," he said.

"No—" I said.

"Now you're in a world where you don't belong. And it's your fault. All your fault."

"How do you know?" I screamed. "What makes you the expert? How do you know anything about me?"

"Because I *am* you!" he shouted back. "I'm Ross Arthur in this reality, in this world. And you don't belong here! You're an Intruder. A dangerous Intruder. You can't stay!"

"No!" I cried again. "You're not Ross—I am!" I screamed.

But I knew I didn't belong here.

I couldn't belong here. Too many weird things had happened. Things I couldn't explain.

My twin said I broke the fabric of reality. But that sounded totally crazy.

Was I really in a parallel world?

My head began to throb. I didn't know what to believe.

"You have to go," my twin ordered. "Get out— now!"

"GO? Where am I supposed to go?" I shouted. "I'm staying. You leave!"

And then I lost it.

I jumped on him. In a wild fury, I grabbed him around the neck.

I dropped him to the floor.

I kicked him hard in the stomach.

With an angry groan, he rolled on top of me. Punched me in the chest.

And we wrestled, wrestled frantically, rolling over the floor, punching, clawing, pounding each other.

"Only one of us belongs here, Ross," he gasped. "Only one of us can stay. Me! You can't survive here! I'm telling the truth. You can't survive. You're going to die!"

I wrapped my twin in a headlock. I tightened my grip until his face turned red.

"I'm not going to die!" I gasped.

He twisted free and slammed me to the floor. He jumped on top of me and started to twist my arm.

"Owwwwww." I let out a howl of pain.

A hard knock on the bedroom door made us both stop. We were wheezing, choking, gasping for breath. My side ached. My head throbbed. My neck was stiff.

He had a deep, red scratch down his left arm.

"Ross, what on earth are you and Jake doing in there?" Mom called in.

"Uh . . . nothing," my twin answered, wiping a gob of spit off his chin. "We're just . . . kidding around."

"No! Mom, help me!" I cried. "It's me! Please! Open the door! I—"

My twin clamped his hand over my mouth before I could say more. He furiously motioned for me to be quiet.

I struggled to get free.

My twin clamped his hand tighter over my mouth. I couldn't move. I couldn't make a sound.

Please, open the door! I silently begged. Please, Mom!

But the door remained closed. "Just don't wreck your room. It was cleaned this morning," Mom called in.

"No problem," my twin answered.

We listened to her footsteps padding down the stairs.

When she was gone, my twin finally lifted his hand from my mouth. "That was very stupid," he muttered. "She wouldn't help you. She would know instantly that you don't belong here."

"What are you saying?" I cried weakly.

I pulled myself to a sitting position on the floor and leaned my head against the bed.

"You just don't get it, do you," he said.

I wiped sweat off my forehead with the sleeve of my T-shirt. "Get what?"

"You don't understand what is happening here," he said, rubbing the red scratch on his arm. "You really never studied parallel worlds?"

I shook my head.

"Well, there are many, many parallel worlds," he said. "I live in one world, and you live in another."

"You live in the world of the cuckoos," I muttered.

He sighed and continued. "That night at Max's

party, the portal between our worlds opened up."

I frowned at him. "You mean in the swimming pool?"

He nodded. "I saw you there in the water. I couldn't believe what I was seeing. I was so scared. It took me a while to figure out what had happened."

"What happened?" I asked.

"You slipped into my world, Ross. You slipped through the portal. You swam into my world."

I rolled my eyes. Something weird was definitely going on. But portals? Parallel worlds? "I don't think so," I said.

He jumped to his feet. "I'm trying to explain," he snapped. "I'm sure it looked to you like your world. The people were all the same. The places were all the same. But it's different in a lot of ways. It's a parallel world. It's my world."

"Tell me another one," I muttered.

This guy was as good a liar as I was! He was so good, he almost had me believing him.

"Since that night at Max's party," he continued, "you've been slipping in and out of my world. You've been going back and forth between our worlds. And now you seem to be stuck here. But you can't stay in this reality. You don't belong."

"Then why don't *you* leave?" I shot back.

All this talk about parallel worlds was starting to give me the creeps.

"You don't belong," he repeated. "And you . . .

you can do a lot of damage."

I swallowed hard. "Huh? What do you mean?"

"You are from another world. You can't just barge in and interfere with our world. You are dangerous. You are an Intruder. That's what we call people like you."

An Intruder?

"Intruders are very dangerous," my twin continued. "Even if they don't mean to be. Sometimes when they touch things, they change them. Sometimes they destroy things completely."

"Okay. I get it," I said. "I'm an Intruder. If I touch something, I destroy it."

"You believe me?" he asked.

"Yes," I replied.

I crossed the room and grabbed him with both hands.

"Goodbye!" I shouted. "Goodbye!"

He jumped up and shoved me away. "Nice try," he muttered. "But you can't control it. You can't just grab people and destroy them any time you want."

He glared at me angrily. He balled his hands into fists. "Don't ever try anything like that again," he said.

And then he lowered his voice. "But there isn't much point in worrying about you. You're going to die in a day or two."

"You're crazy," I muttered, breathing hard. I balled my hands into fists, too. I was ready to fight again if I had to.

"Haven't you already started to feel the pain?" he asked. "The pain of being in a world where you don't belong? Intruders always feel more and more pain."

I swallowed hard. The headaches? The powerful, stabbing headaches I'd had this afternoon? Is that what he was talking about?

No way. Everyone gets headaches from time to time.

"And when the pain becomes unbearable, Intruders start to fade away," my twin continued. "They get lighter and lighter . . . they fade until you can see right through them . . . lighter and lighter . . . until they blow away like a dead leaf."

"Nooooo!" A scream of protest burst from my throat. "You're crazy! You're a liar!"

A crooked smile spread slowly over my twin's face. "You'll see," he murmured.

"No!" I shouted again. "No—you'll see!"

I lowered my shoulder and rammed right into him, shoving him hard. He let out a startled cry and toppled onto the bed.

By the time he regained his feet, I had the bedroom door open and burst out into the hall.

"Mom! Mom—help me!" I shouted, running to the stairs.

I leaped down the stairs, two at a time. "Mom! Where are you?"

I ran through the house, calling for her. Back to the gym. Down to the family room. No sign of her.

I peered into the garage. Her car was gone. She must have gone out, I realized.

My heart pounding, I ran out onto the driveway. I've got to get away from here, I decided. I've got to get away and think.

I took off, running across front lawns. It was a hot, smoggy L.A. night. The air felt heavy and wet. I was already sweating. My shoes thudded over the perfectly trimmed lawns.

A Jeep rolled past, music blaring out the window. Its headlights rolled over me as it passed.

Normal. Everything normal.

Max's house came into view on the other side of the long, low hedges. Maybe Max is home, I thought. Maybe I'll stop in and see what's up with him. Try to talk to him. Maybe he can help me figure out what's really going on.

I ducked through the spot in the hedge that I always use. The backyard was dark. One terrace light on at the garage. The house was dark, too.

No one home, I decided. I wiped sweat off my forehead. Despite the heat of the night, I felt chilled. The back of my neck tingled. I'm just tense, I decided.

I started back toward the street but stopped when I heard a sharp yip. I turned and saw Flash, the O'Connors' Dalmatian, come trotting across the grass.

"Flash!" I called. I was glad to see him. I'd known Flash since he was a puppy.

The O'Connors live across the street. Sometimes when they go on vacation, we take Flash to our house. "Hey, Flash—how's it going?"

The dog stopped suddenly, a few feet from me. He began sniffing the air furiously. His ears perked straight up.

"Hey—Flash?" I called. I knelt down and motioned for him to come get some hugs. "Here, boy. Come on, boy."

To my surprise, the dog lowered his head—and started to snarl.

"Hey—" I jumped to my feet.

Flash pulled back his lips, revealing two rows of sharp teeth. He snarled menacingly, his entire body arched, tense.

"Flash—it's me!"

With a furious growl, the big dog leaped at me.

I dodged to the side. Lost my balance. Slid on the grass. Landed hard on my side.

The snarling dog turned. Eyes red. White drool making the sharp teeth glisten.

He uttered another angry growl. Leaped hard. Lowered his head—and sank his teeth into my arm.

I let out a howl of pain and tried to roll away.

But the dog was too heavy, too strong.

Pain shot down my arm, my entire side.

With a groan I reached up both arms and grabbed the dog around the neck. I shot my hands forward, struggling to pull the furious Dalmatian off me.

He snapped his jaws angrily, snarling, clawing at me.

I held on to his neck. Held on tight, trying to push him away.

And then suddenly he uttered a high, soft cry. Like the mew of a cat.

Flash's red eyes appeared to dim. He backed off me, staggered back. He raised his head and opened his mouth wide in a high, shrill howl. A howl of pain.

I rolled away. Stumbled to my feet, gasping for breath, rubbing my throbbing arm.

And I saw the white fur on Flash's neck. Saw it blacken. Saw the red handprints on the dog's bare skin.

And then Flash uttered a choking sound. A gurgling from deep in his throat.

He gazed up at me—no longer angry, but surprised. Confused.

The fur fell off his body. And his skin peeled. Flaked away.

"Ohhhhhh." A moan of horror escaped my throat as the dog toppled onto its side.

It dropped heavily onto the grass and didn't move again.

And its skin—its skin and fur—melted away as I stared down at the lifeless form.

"No!" I cried. I knelt down and grabbed the dog in my hands. "Flash! Flash!"

His skin peeled off in my hands. Warm, wet chunks of skin.

I gagged. Jumped away, frantically wiping my hands on my jeans.

The dog's skin all melted away until I was staring at the gray skeleton. Shimmering in the light from the low half moon, gray rib bones curling up from the grass. And an eyeless, silvery dog skull, jaw open in a silent cry.

I did this!

The words rang in my ears.

I did this to Flash!

No. I didn't want to hear it. I didn't want to believe it.

Holding my hands over my ears, I turned and ran. Ran without seeing. Ran without thinking.

The dog's last pitiful howl repeated in my ears. I

kept running as if trying to escape from it, to escape from the sound in my own head.

I don't know how long I ran. I suddenly found myself on Rodeo Drive. The classy shops were all closed. The sidewalks were empty, except for a few window-shoppers, peering into the brightly lit store windows.

I stopped running. I was drenched in sweat, my hair matted to my head. My T-shirt stuck to my body. My chest ached from running for so long.

I leaned in a doorway and gazed down the street. It all looked normal to me. The shops, the restaurants. The same as always.

I stepped away from the building when I heard shouts. Angry, excited shouts. Across Wilshire Boulevard, a block away.

I crossed Wilshire, followed the voices—and found myself on a street lined with small stores. They were all closed. The sidewalk was deserted—except for the shouting men.

Three L.A. cops surrounded a young man. Two of the cops held the guy tightly by his arms. The third cop stood in front of the guy, blocking my view of him.

What's going on? I wondered.

I ducked behind the trunk of a huge palm tree and watched from my hiding place.

The cops were wearing uniforms I'd never seen before. Uniforms that looked like spacesuits, shiny silver and padded, and helmets just like the ones astronauts wear. Weird.

"Looks like we caught one," one of the cops said.

"Yep. He's an Intruder," another one said excitedly. "I've never seen one—have you?"

"No. But let's keep this quiet," he answered. "We don't want the neighborhood in a panic."

I moved in the shadows. Ducked behind another tree to get a closer look.

Finally I could see the young man. He had long, blond hair. Wild, blue eyes. A tattoo snaking along one arm.

He was struggling to free himself from the two cops who held him. Bending and twisting. He started screaming at the top of his lungs, his hair flying up, head tossed back.

"I'm not an Intruder!" he shrieked. "I'm not! You've got the wrong guy!"

The cops weren't buying it. "Calm down," one of them said. "Save your strength."

"Why fight?" the other cop shouted. "You don't have much time."

"Give up."

Instead, the man lurched forward with a furious cry, struggling to burst free.

The two cops lost their hold for a moment. Crying out, they made a wild grab for him. And ripped off the man's sport shirt.

One of the cops screamed. Another one shut his eyes and turned away.

I gaped in amazement at the man's bare chest. I could see his heart pumping inside him . . . see his stomach churning and bobbing . . . see blue blood pulsing through his veins, his guts twisting and curling.

I could see right through him!

Suddenly the man doubled over. He uttered gasp after gasp. The light faded from his eyes. He hugged himself tightly. "The pain . . ." he moaned. "Ohhhh, help me. I can't stand the pain."

His screams and cries rang in my ears. My head started to throb.

I shrank back. Pressed myself against the tree. I shut my eyes and covered my face with my hands.

It was all true, I realized.

My twin had told the truth about Intruders. He had told the truth about me.

I didn't belong here. I was an Intruder, too.

And in a day or two . . . in a day or two . . .

I'd be gone. Forever.

The cops shoved the poor Intruder into the back of a van. The van sped off quietly. No flashing lights. No siren.

I was the only one on the sidewalk. I felt paralyzed, frozen with fear.

How could I save myself? How could I return to my own world before I faded away?

My head felt ready to burst. My panic made my heart leap around in my chest.

How did I get here in the first place? I asked myself.

The portal . . . The portal . . .

"Whoa!" I let out a cry. My twin had already told me the answer. It was so simple!

Max's swimming pool! That's where he and I had seen each other for the first time. That's the portal between our two worlds!

I had just been there a few minutes ago, in Max's backyard. I was so close . . . so close to returning home . . . and didn't even realize it.

Yes!

I pumped both fists in the air. I let out a happy shout.

I turned and made my way back across Wilshire Boulevard. Back down Rodeo Drive. I knew what I had to do. It was so clear, so easy.

I'll return to Max's backyard, I told myself. And I'll jump into the pool. Clothes and all. I'll dive down . . . swim underwater . . . through the portal . . . swim back to my world.

I'm so lucky, I decided.

I figured out how to return home before I got too weak. Before I started to fade away. Before the pain became unbearable.

So lucky . . .

I was just a block from Max's house, walking fast, swinging my arms, when the black-and-white police cruiser pulled up beside me.

"Stop right there," a gruff voice barked.

I froze. A cold shudder shook my body.

Panic choked my throat. My knees felt about to collapse.

They know!

They know I'm an Intruder!

How did they find out?

A round-faced cop with a flat buzz cut and tiny, round black eyes leaned his head out of the patrol car. "Where you headed, son?" His tiny eyes studied me up and down.

"H-home," I choked out.

He frowned and kept his eyes locked on me. "You live around here? Or are you out sight-seeing?"

"No. I live down there." I pointed. I told him the address.

"What's your name, son?" The radio in the car squawked loudly. A low voice on the radio was calling out numbers. "Do you have any ID?"

"ID? N-no," I stammered. I reached for my back pocket. "I left my wallet at home. But I'm Ross

Arthur. My Dad is Garrison Arthur. He's with Mango Pictures."

"We don't need your family history," the cop's partner said from behind the wheel. "You shouldn't be walking around at night, kid."

He turned to the other cop. "Let's go. We've got a 308 on Sunset."

They sped away without saying good-bye.

I stood there trembling, watching the patrol car whirl around the corner. I hugged myself to stop the shaking. Cold sweat clung to my forehead, my cheeks.

A close call, I knew.

I have to get out of here, I told myself. I won't be safe for a second—until I get back to my own world.

I took off running. I didn't stop until I got to Max's house.

I was halfway up the front lawn when I saw the dog skeleton poking up from the grass near the hedge. The pile of bones gleamed dully under the moonlight. The ugly sight made my stomach lurch.

Poor Flash.

I've got to get home before I harm anything else, I told myself.

Max's house was dark except for a porch light. Still no one home.

I made my way along the side of the house to the back. A dim yellow light spilled out from one of the bedrooms. Otherwise, I moved through total darkness.

I stepped onto the terrace in back. My heart started to pound with excitement.

I was so hot and drenched with sweat. I could use a cold swim.

Especially a swim that would bring me home.

I'll jump into the shallow end and swim toward the deep water, I told myself. Just as I did that night at Max's party.

I'll swim to the deep end . . . slip through the portal . . . and be out of this frightening world forever.

My shoes scraped the stone terrace as I jogged to the pool.

I stepped eagerly to the edge. Peered down.

And stared at bare concrete.

"No! No! No!" I pounded my fists against my sides.

The pool had been drained.

I had no choice. There was no water in the pool, and I was out of ideas. I had to go back to my twin's house. I had to talk to him. He was the only one who might be able to help me.

I sneaked in through the back door and crept upstairs to his room. He looked up from his computer as I walked in, and flashed me a disgusted scowl. "You're back?" he sneered.

He stood up, walked to the window, and gazed out into the blackening night.

From far in the distance I heard the shrill call of a bird, a strange, trilling sound I'd never heard before.

A sound from a different world.

A different reality.

"You've got to help me," I pleaded. "Tell me, how . . . how do I get back to my world? What do I have to do?"

He turned slowly and stared at me for a long while. Finally he snickered coldly. "I don't know. It's your problem."

"No!" I cried. I jumped up and crossed the room

to him. I grabbed him by the front of his T-shirt. "You have to know!" I screamed. "You have to know!"

He pulled free and stumbled away from me. "I— I don't want to fight again," he said.

"Then tell me!" I demanded. "You know all about this—right? You studied it in the fourth grade. You know about portals and parallel worlds. You know it all—don't you?"

I backed him into a corner.

He tensed his body. Raised his hands, as if expecting another fight.

"Tell me!" I screamed.

"Okay, okay," he replied, motioning with both hands for me to back off. "Just sit down, okay? I think I know how you can do it. But stop screaming."

Breathing hard, I took a few steps back. "Tell me," I demanded again.

"Okay. Sit down," he said. "You've been a liar your whole life, right?"

I glared at him. "Excuse me?"

"Just go with me on this," he said. "You've been a liar your whole life."

"Whatever," I muttered. And then I snapped, "How do you know?"

"I already told you. Because I'm you," he replied. "You slipped into my world because your whole world became a lie, okay? If you want to get back to your world, you have to reverse it."

I scratched my head. "Huh? Reverse it?"

He nodded. "Yeah. You have to tell the truth. You have to tell the truth to someone about what has happened to you."

I swallowed. "You mean I have to explain to someone from your world that I'm an Intruder? That I came here from another world?"

"Yes. And you have to make them believe you." he said.

"But—everyone knows I'm a liar!" I cried. "Everyone knows I make up stories all the time. Who would believe me? Who?"

He shrugged. "Beats me."

And suddenly, I had an idea.

"Where can I sleep tonight?" I asked.

My twin yawned. "I don't care. Go sleep in a tree."

"Can I sleep on the floor?" I asked.

He shrugged. "Do what you want. Just leave me alone."

A short while later my twin clicked off the lights and climbed into bed. I struggled to get comfortable on the rug.

We live in different worlds, I thought. But our lives are a lot alike.

If his Mom was like mine, she would get up early. And she would go into the kitchen to make coffee and call her friend Stella, who also gets up early.

And if I came downstairs while my twin was still asleep, I could talk to her. And I could quietly, calmly explain the whole thing.

Then I would bring her upstairs—and she'd see the proof. Two Rosses!

This is going to work. I'm practically home, I

thought as I drifted off to sleep.

When I woke up, gray morning light filled the window. I raised my head and squinted at the clock-radio beside the bed. Six-ten.

I had overslept a little. But it was okay.

My twin was sound asleep on his stomach, covers pulled up to his head.

If he was like me, his alarm wouldn't go off for another hour.

Yawning silently, I dragged myself to my feet. My back ached from lying on the hard floor. I'd slept in my underwear. I pulled on my jeans and T-shirt from yesterday.

I bent to tie my sneakers. Then I crept out of the room on tiptoes, and down the stairs to the kitchen.

The aroma of fresh coffee floated out to greet me. The kitchen was dark, except for the pale gray light from the windows.

Mom sat with her back to me on a tall stool at the counter. She had a white mug of coffee steaming beside her. The telephone was pressed to her ear.

The same Mom, I thought. The same blue bathrobe. Her hair unbrushed. One blue slipper on her foot, the other on the floor.

"I know, I know," she was saying into the phone. "Stella, tell me something I don't already know. Nothing changes. Really."

I tapped her on the shoulder.

A mistake.

She let out a startled squeal and dropped the phone. "Ross—what on earth!"

"Sorry, Mom," I said softly.

"What are you doing up so early? You scared me to death!" Mom exclaimed.

She picked up the phone and returned it to her ear. "Sorry, Stella. It was Ross. What were you saying?"

"I want to tell you something," I said. "Something kind of crazy."

She shrugged and pointed to the telephone. I could hear Stella's voice at the other end. She sounded like a quacking duck.

"Go make yourself some cereal," Mom whispered, waving me away.

"Okay," I said. "But I need to tell you something."

"I know, I know," she said into the phone. "You're not the only one, Stella. It happens. It happens a lot."

I went to the cabinet. I pulled down a bowl and a box of cornflakes. "I really have to talk to you," I told Mom.

She lowered the phone from her ear. "Stella got another call. She put me on hold. What do you want to tell me?"

"Well . . ." I shoved the cereal box away. I didn't really know where to begin. I knew I had to tell it right. I had to make her believe me.

"Are you in trouble, Ross?" Mom asked, her face wrinkling in concern.

"Well . . . yes and no," I said. "You see, Mom—a strange thing happened to me."

"How strange?" She had the phone pressed to her ear, but she was studying me, her eyes locked on mine.

"Pretty strange," I said. "You see, you're not really my mom. I—"

"Oh, Ross! Not another one of your crazy stories!" she cried. "It's too early! Go back to sleep, okay? You've got another hour to sleep."

"Just listen to me," I said. "I know I've made up a lot of things in the past. But not today. Today I'm really serious, and I really need your help, okay?"

I took a deep breath. I stared at the cereal box. For some reason, I couldn't look at her. I didn't want to see her face in case she didn't believe me.

"Just let me tell the whole thing, Mom. And please believe me," I begged. "Please. I'm not making this up."

I stared at the cereal box. "The portal was open, and I slipped into a parallel world," I continued. "You probably know all about parallel worlds. Ross—I mean, the other Ross, your Ross—said he studied them in school. Well, that's what happened to me."

I took a deep breath. "I'm Ross, but I'm not the same Ross you know. I belong in a different world. I'm what you call an Intruder. And I need to get back there fast. I need you to believe me, Mom, so I can get back there. If you come upstairs, I can prove it to you. The other Ross—your Ross—is still in bed. Sleeping."

Whew. I got it all out.

I took a deep breath and hesitantly raised my eyes from the cereal box to Mom. "Do you believe me?" I asked in a whisper. "Do you? Will you come upstairs?"

I held my breath. "Mom?"

She hung up the phone. "What is it, Ross?" she snapped.

"Do you believe me?" I repeated.

"Believe what? I have to run over to Stella's house. She's very upset."

She waved me away. She hadn't heard a word I said.

"Just stop in my room before you get dressed," I begged. "I have something to show you. It's an emergency!"

"I'm not getting dressed, Ross. I'm only going next door." Mom grabbed her raincoat from the coat closet and threw it over her bathrobe. "Stella has an emergency. A real emergency. She doesn't make up stories."

Mom stepped out the back door. I watched her hurry across the lawn to Stella's house.

I sighed and slumped out of the room. Strike one.

I trudged back upstairs to my room. My twin was

still sound asleep. He had kicked all the covers onto the floor. I do that sometimes, too.

I suddenly felt so homesick. I wanted to be back safe and sound in my real room. I wondered what my real mom was doing. I wondered if the real Jake was awake yet.

I stood over the bed and stared at my twin for a long moment. It felt so weird to see myself, how I looked, how I slept. He was me in every way.

And this was his room. I didn't belong here. And if I didn't find someone to believe my story, I wouldn't be here much longer.

"Wake up," I whispered. I bent down and shook him by the shoulders. "Come on. Wake up."

He blinked one eyelid open. "Huh? What's your problem?" he asked, hoarse from sleep. "What time is it?"

"It's early," I said. "But I don't have much time. I want to go to school with you."

He opened his other eye. "Excuse me?"

"I have to find someone to believe my story. So I have to go to school with you. As soon as my friends—your friends—see the two of us, they'll believe me. I know they will."

He sat up sharply. "No way," he said.

"Huh? You won't let me go to school?" I cried.

"Of course I'll let you go to school." A slow smile spread across my twin's face. "But I'm not going with you. You're going to have to make someone believe you all by yourself. No way I'm helping." He let out a loud yawn.

"Fine. I'm going to school now," I said. "I'm going to school—and I'm going to make someone believe me."

I stepped out into a warm, smoggy day. The air already heavy and damp. Along the block, gardeners were unloading their trucks. A woman in a gray maid's uniform was walking two white standard poodles along the curb.

It seems so much like home, I thought sadly. But I guess I'm as far away from home as a person can be.

I didn't have much time to feel sorry for myself. I saw Cindy on the next block, and I ran to catch up with her.

"Hey, wait up! Cindy—wait up!"

She was riding her bike, pedaling hard, her black hair bobbing behind her.

"Hey, wait!"

She finally stopped and turned around. "Ross? What's up?"

I ran over to her. "I have to tell you something," I said breathlessly.

She started pedaling again. "We're late. What is it, Ross?"

"I'm not really Ross," I said, struggling to keep up. "I'm Ross in a different world. And I have to get back there."

"You have to get back to the insane asylum!" She laughed. "You and your crazy stories."

"Cindy—please," I begged. "I'm not kidding about this. I'm really, really, really serious."

Her smile faded. "I don't get it. What's the joke?"

"It's not a joke," I said. "I don't belong here. I can't stay in this world. I have to get back to where I belong. If I don't . . ." My voice cracked.

"All I need is for you to believe me," I pleaded. "To believe what I'm telling you."

She rolled her eyes. "You want me to believe that you're an alien from another planet?"

"No!" I cried. "I want you to believe that I'm Ross in a parallel universe. I—I'm an Intruder!"

As she stared at me, her eyes darted back and forth. I could see she was thinking hard, trying to decide.

I crossed my fingers behind my back. "Do you believe me, Cindy?" I asked. "Do you?"

"Okay," she said finally. "Okay. I believe you."

"Great!" I cried. "Thank you! Thank you!"

"I also believe that the moon is made of Limburger cheese," Cindy said. "And I believe that I can flap my arms and fly to Mars anytime I want." She burst out laughing.

"Wait! I can prove it to you!" I said.

I don't know why I didn't think of this before. But I could show Cindy that I was an Intruder!

"Watch this!" I said. I fell onto the grass, landing on my back. "Intruders destroy things. Right?"

Cindy just rolled her eyes.

"When I get up, the grass will burn and sizzle. You'll see."

I pressed my back hard into the grass. I wanted to make sure the grass turned totally brown.

I stood up. "Okay. Look."

We both stared down at the ground.

"Whoa." Cindy's eyes opened wide. "That's unbelievable. Flat grass."

Flat grass. That was it. The grass lay flat where I

had fallen. Still green. Not burned at all.

Why didn't it work this time? I wondered, staring at the grass. My twin could probably tell me, but it really didn't matter now.

The only thing that mattered was making Cindy believe me.

"Cindy—" I glanced up, but she was gone. I watched her pedal away, bumping over the curb, onto the next block. "I'm not giving up," I said out loud. "No way."

But a sharp stab of pain made me grab my head. I shut my eyes, trying to force the pain away.

"Ohhh," I groaned as my stomach started to ache. I bent over as the pain increased, as if thousands of razors pierced my stomach. The pain was so intense, I couldn't walk.

I hunched at the curb, doubled over in agony. My head. My stomach. It's happening, I realized. Just as my twin predicted. The horrible pain . . .

I forced myself to walk to school. I knew I didn't have much time. I had to find someone to believe my story.

I tried Max next. I found him at his locker across from Miss Douglas's class. "Max, listen to me," I said. "I'm an Intruder. I'm not really Ross."

He laughed. "Whatever," he said, and started toward class.

"Max—wait!" I called. "Please! If I told you a totally wild, totally insane story about me slipping between parallel worlds . . . if I told you that I'm not really the Ross you know, and that I don't belong here in your world . . . if I swore it was all true . . . would you believe me? Is there any chance at all you would believe me?"

He opened his mouth to answer. "No way—" he started.

"Think about it," I said. "Don't answer right away. Think about it, okay?"

He nodded. "I've thought about it."

"And?" I asked.

"And I think you're trying to get out of helping me wash my father's car," he said. "Nice try. But it won't work. You promised. See you after school. And don't forget to bring the car wax."

"Max—why won't you believe me?" I shouted.

"Everyone knows your crazy stories, Ross," he said grinning. "Everyone."

The bell rang.

Max shouted goodbye and hurried down the hall to class. I watched him for a moment, his words repeating in my mind.

Words of doom.

I could feel panic tighten my throat. My legs shook again as I slumped into Miss Douglas's classroom. I saw her standing at the side of her desk, straightening a pile of papers.

And suddenly I realized: She has to believe me.

She's a teacher. She has to believe her students.

If I beg her to believe me, she'll see how desperate I am. She won't be like my friends and think it's all a big joke.

Because why would I joke with a teacher? And I bet she knows all about parallel worlds.

I began to feel hopeful again. Just a little hope. But enough to make me think I might be able to return home after all.

"Miss Douglas!" I called.

Eyes turned as I tossed my backpack to the floor and took off running to the front of the room.

"Miss Douglas! Can I tell you something?"

Miss Douglas didn't believe me, either.

She thought I was trying to get out of taking a test. "But I have to admit this is one of your better stories, Ross," she snickered, shaking her head.

"Go take your seat," she said, waving me away. "I'm sure you'll have an even better story for me tomorrow."

I trudged across the room to my desk.

There won't be a tomorrow, I thought bitterly.

There won't be a tomorrow for me because no one will believe me.

So what if I'm a liar? So what if I make up stories all the time?

Why can't someone believe me when I do tell the truth?

After class I tried to stand up. But I felt weak. I could feel my strength draining away.

My backpack suddenly weighed a ton. It took real effort to raise my shoes from the floor and make my way to my next class.

No one is going to believe me, I realized. Even my teacher thinks it's a big joke.

But I knew I had to keep trying.

In line at the lunchroom I asked one of the lunch servers if she believed in parallel worlds. She stared at me and asked if I wanted pizza or macaroni.

I looked for Sharma. But some kids told me she and her family went away for a few days.

After school I told my story to the tennis team coach. Coach Melvin listened silently, squeezing a tennis ball in one hand.

When I finished, he thought for a moment. Then he said, "I once had a dream like that. You can skip practice today, Ross, if you're upset about your dream."

He hurried off to start practice.

With a sigh I tried to sling my tennis racket onto my shoulder. But I didn't have the strength. I couldn't raise it that high.

My backpack felt too heavy to carry. My legs felt so weak, I kept stumbling on the sidewalk. The wind blew me off the grass onto the curb.

Feeling lost and defeated, I headed for home. It's as good a place to disappear as any, I thought sadly.

My twin greeted me at the front door. "You're back?"

I nodded weakly, struggling to catch my breath. Stomach cramps made it hard to breathe. My head throbbed with pain.

My twin followed me outside. I slumped wearily against a tree.

"You failed, huh?" he said. He had a crooked smile on his face, as if he was enjoying my suffering. "Sorry," he said. "The sun is heading down. I don't think you have much time."

"I . . . know . . ." I whispered.

I stared hard at him. The sinking sun made his face glow. His gray eyes gleamed in the soft light.

I gazed at him, so healthy, so strong, so . . . alive.

And suddenly I had an idea.

Suddenly I knew how I could save myself.

I pointed at the other Ross. "You!" I said.

He took a step back. And narrowed his eyes at me. "Me? What about me?"

"YOU believe me!" I cried. "YOU believe the story. So—I'm safe! You said I need only one person to believe my story—and it's YOU!"

To my surprise, he burst out laughing.

"I've won!" I insisted. "I can go back to my world now."

He shook his head and laughed again.

"What's so funny?" I demanded. "This is serious. I did exactly what you told me to do. I found some-one to believe me. You! You! You! So now I'm safe."

"No, you're not," he replied, still grinning. "I lied."

"You what?" I cried.

"I'm you—remember?" he said. "I'm your exact double, Ross. You're Ross—and I'm Ross. We're the same, right? So . . . sometimes I make up stories."

"You mean . . . you mean . . ." I swallowed hard.

I suddenly felt weaker. I staggered back onto the front lawn. Smacked hard into the tree trunk.

A gust of wind pushed me away. I pressed my back into the trunk.

"You mean . . . that's not the way to return to my world?" I whispered.

He raised a hand to his mouth. "Oops! Guess I made up a little story."

"But—but—that's so cold!" I gasped.

He shrugged. "Whatever. I'm you, remember? I'm you in every way. Except that I belong here, and you don't."

The wind lifted me off my feet. I grabbed the trunk to pull myself back to the ground.

"You're fading away," my twin said. "You're practically gone."

I glanced at my hands. I could see right through them. I could see through my arms.

The wind picked me up again. I dived for the tree trunk and flung my filmy arms around it.

I'm going to blow away, I realized. Like a dead leaf.

I felt so weak . . . weak and drained.

Holding tightly to the tree trunk, I turned to my twin. "Aren't you going to help me?" I pleaded. "Are you just going to let me disappear?"

"I can't help you," he said. "It's too late."

I clung to the tree, but my grip was slipping. In a few seconds I knew I would flutter away. "You've . . . got to . . . help me," I whispered.

My twin crossed his arms over his chest. "I just want you gone, Ross. If I tell you how to get back to your world, you'll only tell more lies. And you'll end up in my world again."

"No!" I whispered. "No. Tell me how to get back. Tell me! Please! I promise—no more lies. I swear! Only the truth!"

"You're lying!" he shouted. "I know you are!"

"No—please!" I begged. "Please—tell me what I can do."

My twin shook his head. "No way."

I lost my grip on the tree. A blast of wind lifted me off my feet.

"I'll never tell another lie!" I swore. My voice came out so weak, I didn't know if he heard me.

"Okay, okay," he muttered. His expression softened. "Okay. I'll give you a break. I can't stand to see another Ross suffer."

"Thank you," I whispered. "Thank you."

He pointed. "See my garage? There's a room above the garage."

"Yes," I said. "An empty room. I know it. I have the same garage."

"Well, that room is a portal," he continued. "It's a passageway between our two worlds."

"Wow," I murmured.

"Climb up to the room and wait for a door to open," my twin instructed. "Go through that door— and you will be home. You will be home and strong again."

"Thank you," I whispered. "Thank you and good-bye. I promise you'll never see me again."

"Better hurry," he replied. "You've only got a few minutes." He turned and started to jog back into the house.

I gazed at the garage. It stood at the edge of the lawn, only twenty or thirty steps away. But to me, it was a mile in the distance.

Could I walk that far?

Was I strong enough to make it to the garage and up to the top room?

If I let go of the tree, will I just blow away like a leaf? I wondered.

My whole body trembled. I knew I had no choice. I had to try for it. It was my only hope.

My last hope.

Slowly, slowly I let my hands slide off the smooth

tree bark. I sank to my knees in the grass.

Should I crawl?

No.

I took a deep, shuddering breath and pulled myself to my feet.

A gust of wind blew against me. I gritted my teeth and leaned into it.

I took a step forward. Then another.

It felt as if the wind was trying to keep me from the garage. But I had to get there.

I lowered my head and pushed forward. I tried to think heavy thoughts.

I'm a ship's anchor, I told myself. I'm an elephant.

Forward. Step by step. Pushing my light body against the steady, stiff breeze.

I'm nearly there, I realized. Just a few more steps.

I uttered a cry as a sharp gust lifted me off the grass. It sent me flying back. A few seconds later I dropped heavily onto the grass.

I'm not going to quit, I told myself. I'm going to get there. I'm going to get to the portal.

I leaned forward again, lowering my head and shoulders—and trudged ahead. One step. Another. Another.

Breathing hard, my chest heaving from the effort, I stepped into the cool darkness of the garage.

I hugged myself, trying to stop my trembling. And peered at the stairs, half-hidden in darkness at the back wall.

The stairs to the portal between our worlds.

The portal . . . the portal . . .

"NO!" I let out a hoarse, angry scream. "NO! NO!"

I shouted in fury—in terror—because I suddenly knew this was wrong.

My twin had lied to me again.

He lied. He lied.

The garage room can't be the portal.

Because I've never been up in the garage room!

I couldn't move from one world to the other from there—since I'd never been there!

"Get up there, Ross!" a voice barked, right behind me.

I turned and saw my twin. His expression was cold, angry. He gave me a hard shove. "Get up there," he repeated. "I don't want anyone to hear your last screams."

"N-no, please—" I begged weakly.

But he gave me another shove. "It will all be over in a few minutes."

I stumbled forward. He moved to block my escape.

I felt so weak. Pain shot up and down my body. I wanted to curl up . . . curl up into a tiny ball and disappear.

But I couldn't give up. I couldn't let him do this to me. I wouldn't!

It wasn't fair. It wasn't right.

"AAAAAAAGH!" With a cry of fury I spun around—and threw myself onto him.

Startled, he stumbled back.

I clung to him, my arms wrapped around his shoulders. I clung to him with all the strength I had left.

"Get off! Get off me!" he shrieked. He backed out of the garage, twisting, turning, trying to pry me off.

But I held on tight, wrestling with him. Struggling against the pain that pulsed over me. Feeling so light . . . so light . . .

He backed across the lawn. He grasped my arms and squeezed them. "Get off me!"

"No!" I whispered. "I won't give up! I want to go home!"

We wrestled over the grass. I gasped for breath. I knew I couldn't hold on much longer.

And suddenly we were at the edge of our swimming pool. Wrestling. Thrashing. Bending and twisting.

I gazed into the water, sparkling so blue under the afternoon sunlight.

And in the gently rippling water, I saw our reflections. Both of our faces, side by side in the shimmering water.

Just like the first time I saw him.

Exactly like the first time we met.

"Go!" my twin screamed, wrestling hard. "Go forever, Ross!"

I couldn't hold on to him any longer. He flung me

off him. I fell into the pool like a sagging inner tube.

But I reached out—and grabbed his arm.

And pulled him in with me.

We both sank into the cold water. Down . . . down . . .

So cold and clear . . . shimmering with a million dots of sunlight . . . so unreal . . .

We stared at each other underwater . . . stared face to face as we had that night . . . gazed with the same eyes at our identical faces . . .

Lower . . . lower into the cold, clear water.

And this time it was me who mouthed the words: *Go away.*

And as I said it, the water began to darken. As if someone had dimmed the lights.

My chest felt about to explode.

My twin faded away. Vanished in the blackening water.

All dark. All dark now.

I swam in blackness. My chest burning. My whole body throbbing.

The horror rose up . . . rose up around me.

For I knew that I had failed . . . failed.

I was fading into the blackness.

Fading away forever.

Choking . . .

I'm choking, I realized. Can't breathe.

I blinked my eyes open. Felt water slide down my cheeks. Stared through a film of water over my eyes.

Am I still underwater?

So dark. Dark as night.

I coughed up water. Choked and gagged.

Tried to blink the water from my eyes.

And stared up at Cindy and Sharma. Their faces tight with worry. Tears staining Sharma's pale face.

"Hey—he opened his eyes!"

My ears rang. The cry sounded so far away. But I recognized Max's voice.

Cindy leaned over me. "You're okay, Ross," she said in a trembling whisper.

"You're going to be okay," Sharma added.

I opened my eyes wide. I could see clearly now.

I was lying on my back. Staring up at a lot of faces. Beyond the two girls I saw Max and his father. And other kids I knew, all in swimsuits, all huddled together, worried and tense.

Above them the moon floated above a layer of clouds. Night. It was night.

And I was lying on my back on the terrace beside Max's swimming pool.

"I'm so sorry," Cindy said, leaning over me.

"We were just kidding around," Sharma said, holding my arm. "It was supposed to be a joke. We didn't mean to hold you under so long."

"But then you started to choke," Cindy whispered. "It—it was so horrible! You weren't breathing, and—" Her words caught in her throat. She turned away.

"My dad saved your life," Max said.

"It's a good thing I took that CPR class," Max's father said. He leaned over me. "Do you feel okay, Ross?"

"Yeah . . . I guess," I said weakly. I sat up. I was lying in a puddle of cold water.

"We're so sorry," Cindy repeated. "Really, Ross. We didn't mean to hold you under so long. We were so stupid. Please—please forgive us."

The two girls went on apologizing, but I wasn't listening.

I was thinking about my parallel world adventure. Was it all a crazy dream?

It had to be.

It all never happened. I was drowning and my mind hallucinated the whole thing.

I breathed a long sigh of relief and jumped to my feet.

I felt so happy—so happy to be alive, to be back with my friends. I ran around and hugged everyone—even Max!

I'm in my world, I thought gleefully. I'm in the real world. And I'm going to stay here!

Everyone started talking and laughing at the same time. The music rang out again. The party was back underway.

I thanked Max's father, said goodbye to Max, and started running through the backyards to my house. I suddenly remembered about Jake.

I had left him all alone. I wasn't supposed to go out.

Was I going to be in major trouble?

I didn't care. I was so happy, so happy to be back!

I burst into the house and ran up to Jake's room. "Hey—" I called. "What's up?"

Jake was sitting on the bed with his back to me. He turned slowly.

And I opened my mouth in a scream of horror.

His face—his face was gone.

I gaped at his skull . . . his gray, rutted, worm-infested skull . . . empty eye sockets staring blankly back at me . . . his jaw open in an evil toothless grin.

My scream choked off in my throat. I staggered back as Jake's laugh rang out from under the ugly skull.

He raised both hands and tugged the skull off. "Gotcha!" he grinned at me.

A mask.

"You're a wimp," Jake said. "You scare like a little baby!"

I didn't care about his dumb joke. I was so happy to see my brother, I hugged him, too.

"Get off me!" he cried. "What's your problem, Ross? Yuck!"

I backed off, laughing.

I'm here! I thought. Here in my normal world.

Normal. Everything normal!

I tossed back my head and let out a joyful shout.

My cry was cut short when I heard voices in the hall.

I turned—and gasped—as two more Jakes stepped into the room!

"N-no—!" I stammered. "It—it isn't possible!"

The three identical boys stared at me as if I was crazy.

Mom burst into the room. "Ross, you didn't go out, did you?" she asked angrily. "I need you to stay home and take care of the triplets."

My mouth dropped open. I couldn't speak.

My eyes went from face to face to face.

I messed up, I told myself. I really messed up.

Somehow, I ended up in another parallel world.

How do I get out of here?

I can't live with three Jakes. I can't! I can't!

"Well?" Mom demanded, hands on her waist. "Are you going to stay home and watch your brothers?"

"Well . . ." I said.

Think fast. Think fast, Ross.

Think of a good story to get yourself out of this!

ABOUT THE AUTHOR

R.L. STINE says he has a great job. "My job is to give kids the CREEPS!" With his scary books, R.L. has terrified kids all over the world. He has sold over 300 million books, making him the best-selling children's author in history.

These days, R.L. is dishing out new frights in his series THE NIGHTMARE ROOM. When he isn't working, he likes to read old mysteries, watch *SpongeBob Squarepants* on TV, and take his dog, Nadine, for long walks around New York City, where he lives with his wife, Jane, and son, Matthew.

"I love taking my readers to scary places," R.L. says. "Do you know the scariest place of all? It's your MIND!"

Take a look at what's ahead in
THE NIGHTMARE ROOM #5
Dear Diary, I'm Dead

"You did what?" Shawn screamed. "Alex, are you totally whacked?"

"I'm going to win this one," I said.

"But you never win a bet with Tessa," Chip said. "How could you bet a hundred dollars?"

We were in Chip's garage after school, tuning up our guitars. The garage had only one electrical outlet, so we could plug in only two amps. That meant that one of us had to play acoustic, even though we all had electric guitars.

"I won't need a hundred dollars," I said, "because I'm going to win."

Sproinnnng.

I broke a string. I let out a groan. "I'll just play without it," I muttered.

Shawn shook his head. "You're crazy, Alex. After what happened with McArthur and the flag . . . "

"That was a sure thing!" I cried. "I should have won that bet!"

Just thinking about it made me angry.

A few weeks ago, I made a deal with Mr. McArthur. He's one of the janitors at school. Except he's not called a janitor. He's called a maintenance engineer.

McArthur is a nice guy. He and I kid around sometimes. So I made a deal with him.

He raises the flag every morning on the flagpole in front of our school. So I paid him five dollars to raise it upside down on Wednesday morning.

Then I dragged Tessa to school early and bet her ten dollars that he would raise the flag upside down.

"You're crazy, Alex," Tessa said, rolling her eyes. "McArthur has never slipped up like that."

He will this morning, I thought happily. I started planning how I'd spend Tessa's ten bucks.

How was I to know that Mrs. Juarez, the principal, would arrive at school just when McArthur was raising the flag?

She came walking up the steps and saw McArthur. So she stopped in front of the pole, raised her hand to her heart, and waited to watch the flag go up.

Of course McArthur chickened out. He raised the flag right-side up.

I didn't blame him. What could he do with her standing right there?

But I had to pay Tessa the ten bucks. And then McArthur said he'd pay me back my five dollars in a week or so. Not a good day.

"It's my turn," I told my two friends. "Tessa has won about three hundred bets in a row. So it's definitely my turn!"

"But why did you bet her that your diary would be more exciting than hers?" Shawn asked.

"Because it will be," I said. "Tessa is real smart and gets perfect grades. That's because all she does is study. She spends all her time on homework and projects for extra credit. She's so totally boring! So her diary can't be exciting. No way!"

"Who's going to decide whose diary is the best?" Chip asked.

"We're going to let Miss Gold decide," I said. "But it won't be a hard choice for her. This is one bet I'm not going to lose."

"Want to bet?" Chip asked.

I squinted across the garage at him. "Excuse me?"

"Bet you five dollars Tessa wins this bet, too."

"You're on!" I said. I slapped him a high-five.

"Count me in," Shawn said. "Five bucks on Tessa."

"You guys are real losers," I groaned. "Let's play. What's the first song?"

"How about 'Purple Haze'?" Chip suggested. "It's our best song."

"It's our only song," I muttered.

We counted off, tapping our feet, and started to play "Purple Haze." We played for about ten seconds, when we heard a loud, crackling pop.

The music stopped and the lights went out.

We'd blown the fuses again.

A short while later, I dragged my guitar case into the house. Mom greeted me at the door. "I've been waiting for you," she said. "I have a surprise."

I tossed my backpack onto the floor. Then I tossed my jacket on top of it.

"Don't tell me. Let me guess," I said. "I'll bet you five dollars it's a puppy. You finally bought me that puppy I asked for when I was six?"

Mom shook her head. "No puppy. You know your dad is allergic."

"He can breathe at work," I said. "Why does he have to breathe at home?"

Mom laughed. She thinks I'm a riot. She laughs at just about everything I say.

"I'll bet five dollars it's . . . a DVD player!" I exclaimed.

Mom shook her head. "No way, Alex. And stop betting every second. That's such a bad habit. Is that why you're broke all the time?"

I didn't answer that question. "What's the surprise?" I asked.

"Come on. I'll show you." Mom pulled me upstairs to my bedroom. I could see she was excited.

She moved behind me and pushed me into the room. "Check it out, Alex!"

I stared at the big desk against the wall. It was made of dark wood and it had two rows of drawers on the sides.

I stepped up to it. The desktop had a million little scratches and cracks in it.

"It . . . it's old!" I said.

"Yes, it's an antique," Mom replied. "Your dad and I found it at that little antiques store on Montrose near the library."

I ran my hand over the old wood. Then I sniffed a couple of times. "It's kind of smelly," I murmured.

"It won't be smelly after we polish it up," Mom said. "It will be like new. It's a beautiful old desk. So big and roomy. You'll have space for your computer and your PlayStation, and all your homework supplies."

"I guess," I said.

Mom gave me a playful shove. "Just say 'Thank you, Mom. It's a nice surprise. I really needed a desk like this.'"

"Thank you, Mom," I repeated. "It's a nice surprise. I really needed a desk like this."

She laughed. "Go ahead. Sit down. Try it out." She wheeled a new desk chair over to the desk. It was chrome and red leather.

"What an awesome chair!" I said. "Does it tilt back? Does it go up and down?"

"Yes, it does everything," Mom said. "It's a thrill ride!"

"Cool!" I dropped into the chair and wheeled it up to the old desk.

The phone rang downstairs. Mom hurried to answer it.

I tilted the chair back. Then I leaned forward, smoothing my hands over the desk's dark wood. I wonder who owned it before me, I thought.

I pulled open the top desk drawer. It jammed at first. I had to tug hard to slide it open. The drawer was empty.

I slid open the next drawer. The next. Both empty. The air inside the drawers was kind of sour smelling.

I leaned down and pulled open the bottom drawer.

"Hey— what's that?"

Something hidden at the back of the drawer. A small, square black book.

I reached in and lifted it from the drawer.

Then I blew the thick layer of dust off the cover and raised it close to see what it was.

A diary!

I stared at the dusty book, turning it over in my hands. What a strange coincidence!

I rubbed my hand over the black leather cover. Then I opened the book and flipped quickly through the pages.

They were completely blank.

I'll use this to write my diary for Miss Gold, I decided. I'll write my first entry tonight. And I'll write it in ink. Miss Gold will like that.

I set the diary down on the desk and thought about what I would write.

First, I'll describe my friends, I decided. Miss Gold said I needed more description, more details. I stared at the old diary and planned what I would say.

I'll start with me. How would I describe myself?

Well, I'm tall and kind of wiry. I have wild brown hair that I hate because it won't stay down. My mom says I'm always fidgeting. I can't sit still. My dad says I talk too fast and too much.

What else? Hmmm . . . I'm kind of smart. I like to hang out with my friends and make them laugh. I'm a pretty good guitar player. I'd like to make a lot of money and get really rich because I'm always broke, and I hate it.

That's enough about me. What about Chip? How would I describe Chip?

Well . . . He's short. He's chubby. He has really short brown hair and a round baby face. He looks about six, even though he's twelve like me.

Chip wears baggy clothes. He likes to wrestle around and pretend to fight. He's always in a good mood, always ready to laugh. He's a terrible guitar player, but he thinks he's Jimi Hendrix.

Shawn is very different from Chip. He's very intense, very serious. He worries a lot. He's not a wimp or anything. He just worries.

Shawn has brown eyes, orangy hair that's almost carrot colored, and lots of freckles. He gets better grades in school than Chip and me because he works a lot harder.

Who else should I describe? Do I have to describe Tessa? Yes, I guess I should. She'll probably pop up in the diary from time to time.

I guess Tessa is kind of cute. But she's so stuck-up, who cares?

She has straight blond hair, green eyes, a turned-up nose like an elf nose, and a little red heart-shaped mouth. She's very preppy and perfect-looking.

Yes. That's good. Tessa wants to be perfect all the time. And she hangs out only with girls who are just like her.

I flipped through the empty diary one more time. I'm pretty good at description, I decided. I couldn't wait to write this stuff down.

And what else should I write about? I'll write about how my parents bought me a new desk, and how I found a blank diary in the bottom drawer just when I needed a diary. Very cool!

I leaned back in the new desk chair, very pleased with myself. I tilted the chair back a few times. Then I raised and lowered the seat, just to see how it worked.

I heard Dad come home. Then I heard Mom calling me to dinner. I tucked the diary into the top desk drawer and hurried down to the dining room.

"How's the new desk?" Dad asked.

"Excellent," I told him. "Thanks, Dad."

He passed the bowl of spaghetti. "Did you have band practice this afternoon?"

"Yes, kind of," I replied. "We blew the fuses again. We really need a better place to rehearse."

Mom chuckled. "Your band needs a lot of things. Like a singer, for example. None of you guys can sing a note. And how about someone who doesn't play guitar?"

I rolled my eyes. "Thanks for the encouragement, Mom."

Dad laughed, too. "What do you call your band? Strings and More Strings?"

"Ha-ha," I said. Dad has such a lame sense of humor. He's not even as funny as Shawn, who is never funny!

"Bet you ten dollars that we get good enough to win the junior high talent contest," I said.

"Alex, no betting," Mom said sternly.

They started talking to each other, and I concentrated on my spaghetti and turkey meatballs. We used to have real meatballs. But Mom became a health freak. And now all of our meat is made out of turkey!

After dinner, I practically flew upstairs to get started on my diary. I found a black marker pen to write with. Then I sat down in the new desk chair and pulled the diary out of the drawer.

I'll start with an introduction about how I found the diary, I decided. Then I'll describe my friends and me.

I opened the diary to the first page. And let out a gasp.

The page had been completely blank when I found the book this afternoon. But now it was covered with writing. There was already a diary entry there!

At the top, a date was written: Tuesday, January 16.

"Huh?" I squinted hard at it. Today was Monday the fifteenth.

"This is too weird!" I said out loud.

A diary entry for tomorrow?

My eyes ran over the handwritten words. I couldn't focus. I was too surprised and confused.

And then I uttered another gasp when I made another impossible discovery.

The diary entry was written in my handwriting!

A diary entry for tomorrow in my handwriting? How can that be? I wondered.

My hands were shaking. So I set the open book down on the desktop. Then I leaned over it and eagerly started to read.

DEAR DIARY,

The diary war has started, and I know I'm going to win. I can't wait to see the look on Tessa's face when she has to hand over one hundred big ones to me.

I ran into Tessa in the hall at school, and I started teasing her about our diaries. I said that she and I should share what we're writing—just for fun.

I'll read hers, and she could read mine.

Tessa said no way. She said she doesn't want me stealing her ideas. I said, "Whatever." I was just trying to give her a break and let her see how much better my diary is going to be than hers.

Then I went into geography class, and Mrs. Hoff horrified everyone by giving a surprise test on chapter eight. No one had studied chapter eight. And the test was really hard—two essay questions and twenty multiple choice.

Why does Mrs. Hoff think it's so much fun to surprise us like that?

The diary entry ended there. I stared at the words until they became a blur.

My hands were still shaking. My forehead was chilled by a cold sweat.

My handwriting. And it sounded like the way I wrote.

But how could that be? How did an entry for tomorrow get in there?

I read it again. Then I flipped through the book, turning the pages carefully, scanning each one.

Blank. All blank. The rest of the pages were blank.

I turned back to tomorrow's entry and read it for a third time.

Was it true? It couldn't be—could it?

What if it is? I asked myself. What if Mrs. Hoff does spring a surprise test on us? Then, I'd be the only one who knew about it.

I'd be the only one to pass the test.

I closed the diary and shoved it into the desk drawer. Then I found my geography textbook, opened it to chapter eight, and studied it for the next two hours.

The next morning, I ran into Tessa in the hall outside Mrs. Hoff's room. "Nice shirt, Alex," she sneered, turning up her already-turned-up nose. "Did you puke on it this morning, or is that just the color?"

"I borrowed it from you—remember?" I shot back. Pretty good reply, huh?

"How is your diary coming?" Tessa asked. "Or do you want to give up and just pay me the hundred dollars now?" She waved to two of her friends across the hall, two girls who look just like her.

"My diary is going to be awesome," I said. "I wrote twelve pages in it last night."

I know, I know. That was a lie. I just wanted to see Tessa react.

She sneered at me. "Twelve pages? You don't know that many words!" She laughed at her own joke.

"I have an idea," I said. "Why don't we share each other's diaries?"

She frowned at me. "Excuse me?"

"I'll read your diary, and you can read mine," I

said. "You know. Just for fun."

"Fun?" She made a disgusted face at me, puckering up that tiny heart-shaped mouth. "No way, Alex. I'm not showing you my diary. I don't want you stealing my ideas!"

Oh wow.

Oh wow!

That's just what Tessa said in the diary entry.

Was the diary entry coming true? Was all that it said really going to happen?

I suddenly felt dizzy, weak. How could a book predict the future?

I shook my head hard, trying to shake the dizziness away.

"Alex? Are you okay?" Tessa asked. "You look so weird all of a sudden. What's wrong with you?"

"Uh . . . nothing," I said. "I'm fine."

The bell was about to ring. I gazed into Mrs. Hoff's classroom. It was filling up with kids.

I turned back to Tessa. "Uh . . . you haven't read chapter eight yet, have you?" I asked.

"No. Not yet," Tessa replied. "Why?"

"No reason," I said, trying to hide my grin.

I followed her into the room. I waved to Chip and Shawn. Then I dropped my backpack to the floor and slid into my seat at the back of the room.

Mrs. Hoff was leaning over her desk, shuffling through a pile of folders. She has straight black hair and flour-white skin, and she always wears black.

Some kids call her Hoff the Goth. But I don't think that makes sense, and it doesn't even rhyme.

I sat stiffly in my seat, watching her, tapping my fingers tensely on the desktop. My heart started to race.

Is she going to give the test? I wondered.

Is the rest of the diary entry going to come true?